THE ORIGIN *of* LONELINESS

To John
from John

in analytical friendship

18·7·7

UCL

THE ORIGIN
—— *of* ——
LONELINESS

JOHN MARTIN

IOANNES
ME FECIT

First published in Great Britain in 2004
by IMF Press
21 West Square
London SE11 4SN

© John Martin 2004

The moral right of John Martin to be identified
as author of this work has been asserted in
accordance with the Copyright, Designs and
Patents Act, 1988

A catalogue record for this book is
available from the British Library

ISBN 0 9547382 0 9

Produced by Pagewise
2 Butlers Close
Amersham
Bucks HP6 5PY
info@pagewise.co.uk

Art direction and coordination
Mónica Bratt

Editor
Miriam Richardson

Printed in Great Britain
by Beacon Press

I have struggled with difficulty to achieve honesty and without success. Poems and stories are the closest I have approached.

Most of these pieces have places and times beside them, since moments of time are all we have.

CONTENTS

I

Xocoatl or Bitter Water

The Origin of Loneliness

And I thought Patagonia would be my friend
But no, it did not know me.
On the map there is nothing,
From the air a massive sameness
The land of loneliness
And I would know it
And it me
But No
On the road stood two eagles on the body
    of a hare
And around them a halo
Of other birds as beautiful as the dawn
And Patagonia was rich
And I was alone

El Calafate
11th April 2002

Midnight Light

A week before the midnight sun
When light travels great distances
Close to the earth, low and horizontal
It is filtered of wavelengths
So that at midnight
In the Finnish summer
Every colour is muted by a blue-red hue
Not just for a moment
But for lengths of time
The tug boat in the harbour
Is touched with purple
Like a sea cardinal
With gentle yet solid definition
And optimism of a kind unfelt before

And then at half-past one
The sunrise overwhelms all
With liquid light
That brings clarity
Unknown in the south

Flying Kuopio to Helsinki
16th June 2003, 6.00am

HAVANA

I stood in Hemingway's room
At his high writing table
Looking out over a quiet and sunlit Havana
Roofs of terracotta red
Seen through open slatted windows
And gentle noontime breeze
Red tiled floor warming light
From white and brilliant walls
His manuscript there before me
With changes to a verb
That I might have made

Whilst drinking a mojito
in the Hotel de Ambos Mundos
La Habana
19th October 2002, 12.30pm

Arctic Physics

The pilot put his finger on the dial
Lit by the intensity of the light of the
      Arctic summer
Brilliant and clear at thirty thousand feet
"We are flying at seventy-eight percent of
      Mach one
The air compressed at the curved surfaces
Is already near the speed of sound,
To fly faster would damage the skin"

And yesterday
I stood
By the smooth round rock
The size of a whale's hump
Covered with dripping greenness
The air deliciously crisp and wet
As I drank it into my body,
Tumbling in vortices through my lungs,
Surrounded by the silent forest
And I touched the groove
In the smooth rock

That admitted the tip of my finger
And I ran it along
From East to West
Delighting in the smoothness of my passage
Feeling my finger
Clasped by the long line
Gouged in the rock
By that stone
The size of my finger
Moving with massive slowness
Across its curving surface
Trapped under a mile
Of advancing ice
Ten thousand years ago

*Flying from London to Helsinki, in the cockpit
and remembering a rock in the Lake District*

The Yellow Book

Dave, the second officer, turned to me with a grin: "It used to be called the 'emergency procedures book', but they changed the name to 'the yellow book' so it wouldn't frighten us." He explained that "disagree" seen on the aircraft computer screen means a problem and that "LE struts" means "leading edge struts", a part of the aircraft wing that has to be extended for landing.

Landing

"Disagree", green on the screen
"LE struts Disagree"
"Go around Dave" said the Captain
"Helsinki Radar, Speedbird 851 Hotel
We have a technical problem
Permission to go around?"
"Go around Speedbird and good luck"
And Dave grinned at me
And great danger joined with friendship
And I was exhilarated
I was close to the ice on the sea beneath us
To the sunset in our eyes
And to the God that was between us
As we curved into three thousand feet
And the Captain read the yellow book
To Dave

Helsinki
5th January 1996, 4.15 pm

TIERRA DEL FUEGO

In a bar in Tierra del Fuego
The barman asked me if I had heard the news,
That Beckham had a broken foot, today.
And I knew that all was lost
For indeed Manchester United had won

In a bar in Patagonia
10th April 2002

AIRBUS

I was flying from Paris to London in an Air France Airbus early in the morning. The sky was blue behind many small white scattered clouds. About three minutes after take-off when the engines were at maximum whine there was a loud bang. It was full of energy and came from somewhere perhaps below and outside the aircraft. It was a powerful bang. Immediately followed relative quietness and the Airbus levelled out. It flew just under the clouds with the wide green fields of France below. My mind was clear and tense but without anxiety. My first thought was that something had happened to the undercarriage which would mean landing on our belly. That would be exciting. The fellow English passengers around me were unspeaking, eyes catching unknown eyes with the slightest of raising of an eyebrow. Time passed and I felt the intensity of destiny without fear. I remembered the exhilaration of a Chinese battle cruiser locking its missiles on to my helicopter over the South China Sea.

The aircraft was quiet and time passed. Then the captain spoke, not in two languages as before but only in French, in a compact, direct, honest haiku which was perfect and necessary, economical, yet full.

Un réacteur est arrêté
La situation est maîtrisée

A poem had been born. Words of the intensity of the moment, immensely practical yet beautiful conveying technical information yet sensitive to human need. The captain did not intend it as a poem but I recognised it. Perhaps the poet lives continuously at the level of expression that the captain achieved in that moment of passion. The Englishmen around me asked what he had said. And I translated but the words from my mouth in English were not the poem which had existed only at the moment of its saying when it hovered in the cabin and had moved me.

A Poem

Un réacteur est arrêté
La situation est maîtrisée

RAIN

And it rained the rain upon my head
Gentle sweet summer rain
Sea-mountain rain
Bringing happiness and joy in its wetness
Kind running rain on my face
Dripping from my fingertips
And I was with the rain and from the rain,
And the rain was with me.
Norwegian fish girls smiled at me in the rain
And it was our rain
And the wetness thereof was within us
And I welcomed its drops in my eyes
And it flowed from my nose to my lips
It was my rain and I was its man

Bergen
21st August 1993

The Gulf of Finland

I hold the Gulf of Finland in my eyes
Ten thousand feet below
With Finland in my right eye
And Sweden in my left
A myriad of scalloped islands in between.
Soft, gentle, green, edged in ice
Without order or path
Random and dotted, higgled and piggled
And there a single ship within their power
A white line of human order
Cutting through the ice
Science within beauty

Flying Tampere to La Coruña
Gulf of Finland
26th March 1993

Kuopio

In the late morning dawn
All was monochrome
A shade of either black or white
The great light plain
Of the snow on the frozen lake
Carried the dark shadow of a gliding skier
The trees on the islands
Grey and black, with white
And there at the edge
My eye was startled by a single colour
A fringe of brown reeds
Lightly sprinkled with white
Of such delicacy of colour
And lightness of texture
That they would never have been seen
      by man
Except in the monochrome dawn
All was suppressed to show their glory

I kicked the snow
And there below
I met the alien ice

Of startling smoothness
Polished black marble
Without the hand of man
And within its transparent darkness,
Trapped pearls of white snow
As beautiful as the souls of drowned children

Kuopio
7th January 1996

SUMMER TWILIGHT

And the light hovered like a hawk in its waning,
Wherein from one half hour to the next
The same grey gentle long light
Remained, flowing forever continuously
In the northern evening
Long, long, infinitely restrained
Like the white breast of a swan
Reflected in icy water

London
6th June 1993

TIGER

Oh Asiatic Tiger
Lying near my camp
In the night, in the rain
With your eye open
And my eye open

The Jungle, Malaya,
31st December 1990

MALAYA

And I turned in the river
And there he was
The tiger who had looked me in the back
And I was his lord
And he leapt, crashing through shallow waters
Into his jungle
And my friends mocked me
And I retracted
(But I knew it in my heart!)
I convinced myself
(But I knew it in my heart!)
Then the photograph revealed
That he had looked me in the back
As I stood in the river
And I knew it in my heart

Jahor Province, Malaysia
1st January 1991

KUDU

And you see the Kudu bull
And he looks you in the eye
And the grass is high and wet
And the universe is here
For the veldt has no beginning
And it also has no end
All is silent as the grave
Save the smell of sweating brave

Zimbabwe 1988

WARSAW '93

Oh, how beautiful life is!
I heard two Russians singing sad Russian
    songs
With their thin voices in the pale bright
    autumn sunshine
Honest and passionate he put his hand on
    his heart
As I offered him the tattered zlotties

As I walked away
The soft incision of the song followed,
Drawing me to a lingering distance
Where I felt happy yet uncomfortable
With the echo of something unresolved
That I could not grasp

Warsaw
1st October 1993

The Mazurian Lake

Beside a lake in East Prussia
Two fisherman leaned behind a tree
Backing to the horizontal wind
That brought greyness and white
To the scalloped water,
Yellow whiskers at one with yellow reeds
They waited for a hundred pike to fill their net

Then at once, from an unknown place
Brilliant sunshine into the grey
And thirty swans flying
With the white of angels
Bringing power unconceived
Into the heart of man

Wansk
20th March 1995

SUN SHINING

Sun shining, cool and warm
All is bright, I lie quiet
Me, soft entire, unfearing
But best of all a distant tune
Military brass in an unknown place
Bringing waves of optimism
Across the space, to me
Its basis exaggerated by the distance
Ebbing and flowing on the breeze
Evocative, redolent, distant
Abroad, away, yet home and good
Imagined sun on yellow brass
On scarlet jackets, order and roundness
Green palm trees casting fingered shadows.
Onward, established contentment.
I lie face in the pillow
Differentiated, yet as one with all,
Powerful and happily controlled

Quito, Ecuador
26th November 1992

Overhead Greenland

"Hello, Gander this is Speedbird
Zero nine three heavy"
"Hello Speedbird this is Gander,
Proceed from Worbash unto Prawn,
Ascend altimeter three seven two"
"Gander negative, too heavy
I must loose two zero tons"

"Understood my angel heavy,
So ark across the sky"
And men did aviation
And swam into the blue
And lived in three dimensions
Creating geography anew

In the cockpit of a British Airways Boeing 747
North Atlantic
11th October 1994, 1.33 pm

La Rabia

We walked forward in a globe of grey
With our feet on sand unseen
Then ahead and in the sky of greyness
Horizontal lines of waves breaking white,
But high and unexpected, mystical and
　　　frightening

Then from the mist that blocked out all the land
We emerged into a place of joy unknown
Within the centre of our greyish globe
We stood upon an orange plate of sand,
　　　immensely smooth,
Its curvature infinitely small
And shining thin lateral plates of
Grey blue sea sliding over it.
A feeling of a womb from which we came
As small banks of cloud
The size of angels
Ran beside us on the sand

Santillana del Mar
1st May 1995, 3.30 pm

REFLECTIONS FROM A BEACH BELOW

From the angle where I sat at lunch
I saw eight glasses
On a table before the sea
Each glass contained reflected light
(From where I did not see)
So each was filled with orange sand
From a beach below unseen
And when a little wave did break
Upon that unseen distant sand
Each glass was filled with floating white
Upon the orange yellow beach
And behind each glass the blue green sea
For all the rest to see

Santander
Restaurante de Rhin
10th May 1996

NEW YORK[2]

New York is a minimalist abstraction
An immense beauty created by
Either horizontal or perpendicular lines.
But how could man
Who is round and soft
Create such rigid linearity
Unless within himself there is
A minimalist abstraction?

New York
8th July 1993

FLIGHT

Today I have watched
A thousand miles
Of ochre abstract dunes
Pass beneath me
Every line of dunes
With yellow streaks and smudges
To a horizon a hundred miles away
Held at once in my eye
Then the sunset
Over the Timor Sea
And at night
Over the Java Sea
Continuous lightning beside me
As if God had said let there be light
Illuminating spectacular depths of cloud
Seen only at the moment of the discharge
So that vivid massive white structures
Leapt from the blackness
And were gone.

En route Sydney to Singapore
27th November 2003

TRUE ABSTRACTION

Oh train of steel wheels
On steel rails
Of pressure boilers
And hot oiled rods
I look from your windows
And see every yard of county
Over a thousand miles
You and me
Pressed onto the land
For every inch of reality

But plane
You metal tube of thinness
That holds me near to God
With intense white light
Painting brilliance within
And sound unheard on earth
Without
You are true abstraction

London to Sydney
12th November, 2003, local time unknown

Blue Abstraction

Thin shallow water
And me flat within it
Its lateral dimension
Continuous and infinite
Its vertical dimension minimal
Its upper limit air
With sticky interface
Its lower limit sand
Of amorphous shape
Its colour filtered blue

London to Sydney
Thinking about Elba
12th November 2003, local time unknown

BLUE

The blue of the day sea
Itself became translucent green
Before the wave broke
And then lighter green towards the shore
Whose opacity was caused
By a million snow drops of air
Within its smooth smooth depths

But now the plate of sea
Is dark dark with blueness
Till the horizon's sky's
Linear lightness of the blue
Of the eye of a Danish woman
Which moves through
Change without division
To the vertex of the sky
Which is as dark
As the indigo I saw

In the dye-pits of Kano
And which stained my hand
From the belly of the Tuareg

Sydney
15th November 2003, 9.30pm

Xocoatl or Bitter Water[3]

I LOOKED into the lens of the microscope. The view was beautiful. A red blood cell caught my eye, a red bi-concave disc, smooth, round, regular, its edges stained slightly more red than the centre. And the most beautiful of all, placed eccentrically towards the edge of the cell, a blue spot. Its beauty contrasted with its reality. It could only mean one thing, lead poisoning. I lifted my eye from the old brass microscope and looked out of the window down the valley in the high Andes. The whole valley was poisoned with lead.

I was in the surgery of the state dentist at three thousand metres high. It was pitifully equipped, but he was a good man, worried about his patients. He had showed me the mouth of a young woman with the yellow cream of fungus infection under her tongue. "What do you think of her teeth?" I looked closely at her incisors and there was the clinical diagnosis, a black line across both of them at the same level close to the gums. It was lead poisoning. And in an instant I saw the whole picture within her body and within the valley. The lead in her blood had destroyed her body's ability to counteract the growth of the few strands of fungus that we all have in our mouths. They had overwhelmed the resistance of her lead-laden body. This beautiful woman with high mongoloid cheekbones, whose ancestors had crossed the frozen Bering straits ten thousand years ago, would die soon. Would die of ignorance and poverty. Would die of need. Would die of greed.

The income of the valley came mostly from making roof tiles for the whole of the country. At some time in the past one man knew how to make the ochre-red tiles of Spain. Instead of trying to imitate him, others had bought his skill in carts of roof tiles which travelled along colonial roads. It rains on the west of the Andes peaks and the Spanish tiles were porous. The valley had made a glaze with lead that resisted the Andes rain. As I drove back down the valley I saw each home had a pile of old car batteries outside it. These were collected from all over the country, travelling in the reverse direction from the tiles. In each single-roomed house they heated up the batteries on the cooking-fire to extract the lead, whose vapours were breathed by mother, father, grandparents and children. What a disaster of economics and ignorance.

The day before I had been in the capital discussing with the British Council representative what could be done about the high death rate among women during childbirth at high altitude. I had no idea, no hypothesis, no plan. The problem was too difficult. But here was a problem that could be solved by tins of glaze, whose import from Manchester or Shanghai could be encouraged, if someone took control and organised. But what would happen to those who earned their living by bringing car batteries to the valley from hundreds of miles away? What would happen to the price of the tiles? What would happen to the children who would now survive? Driving back to the capital, all passion spent, I was quiet as I closed my eyes to blot out the thousand metre drop beside the unguarded road, and in doing so I saw the blue spot on the red cell still on my retina.

I needed consolation. At a meeting of several valleys and at a lower altitude was a small town with a weekly market where I knew I would find Indians in their tribal dress, each group unique and uniform in bowler hat or white wool shirt. A dress imposed by Spain, now worn with pride. Such is the bad and good of colonialism.

I enjoyed the market. Twenty Indian women in a long row, each selling similar knives, joked with me, with embarrassed smiles turning to laughter as I mimed to them what could be done with their knives. The culmination, a mock lopping off of important parts, generated a universal hilarity, understood to women everywhere. I passed stalls selling dried lama foetuses for magic, potatoes of a hundred different types, some the size of a pea. And then I met her.

She moved along the ground on a small piece of wood under her belly, her hands groping the ground to pull herself along. Her legs dragging without movement behind her. They were small and floppy. It must have been poliomyelitis. Her face looked up to me. I the tallest, straightest man in the town with blue eyes and skin red from high altitude sun looked into her brown face and she into mine. We both smiled at the same moment, spontaneously, effortlessly, with joy and interest. We recognised each other. She stopped and I bent to one knee beside her. "How are you?" And I addressed her in the third person with the respect of the court of Philip the Second and with the accent of Old Castille. And she replied with the dignity of the Ketchua phrase in Spanish.

"What are you doing?" sez I.

"I'm buying things for my children," sez she. And we talked. I talked about my distant land, she about cloth and maize. We liked each other. We were warm together. And then the time came to say goodbye and I rose and turned to go.

"Come back," she said. I turned. "I'm sorry, I lied to you, I don't have any children. I tell people I'm buying for my children because I miss the ones I never had."

"I don't have any children either," I said. And for a moment immense closeness engulfed us, our sadness equal and flowing between us. Too sad even for a tear. "Adiós", "Vaya con Dios".

There in the high Andes I knew that human intimacy was the goal of man and the regret at lost potential was the greatest pain. A pain shared by every one of us; yes, of us, the human beings. The liquid intense clarity of the light, that put nothing between me and the mountains twenty miles away, enhanced my feeling of insight. "Ojalá" came into my lonely mouth. A word I knew in Spanish but not in English. An Arab cry to God in medieval Spain wishing that it were otherwise.

And then another lie was committed. I walked around the market with depth inside me, with quiet strong sadness. Then I saw a man of my own age with his daughter. He a gentle Indian with thick black hair. His daughter about eight or nine holding his hand and looking down at slabs of dark, crude Indian chocolate poured and set on plastic sheets on the ground. The edges of the chocolate smooth and round where they had set hard. And I knew its taste was bitter. The girl's face rose to her father's. Nothing was said but a slight smile and a reserved inclination of her head asked him for chocolate, she already knowing he could not buy it. He shook his head. Oh what pain for me with my pocket full of wealth. How could I intervene? How could I preserve the dignity of the poor father and buy the child chocolate? Or should I leave now letting evolution takes its course?

Reason did not come into decision. Feeling overwhelmed I approached the father. "Forgive me, but today is my birthday and I have no children here to buy chocolate for, would you allow me to buy chocolate for your daughter?" He said nothing but his head nodded. The reserved and fragile child saw me give the chocolate to her father and I saw him give it to his child. And the intensity of my insight was amplified by the clarity of the Andean light.

Naples
June 2003

A Man in New York

NEW YORK was extraordinarily beautiful, and not only for its distant skyline. Within its depths I felt I swam within a tank of abstract beauty. In each direction was living minimalist art: the essence of horizontal and perpendicular lines, carried to every horizon including the sky. Everywhere was radicality. On the pavement a young black man played jazz on the components of a gas cooker. They were distributed around him on the ground. He hit, tickled and excited them, producing the most vigorous percussion I have ever heard. I, a lover of Haydn, stood intoxicated by his primeval, yet sophisticated creation, for half an hour. That night I was assailed by another black man, this time middle-aged, small and thin, yet energetic.

"Come on man, give me a quarter," says he, holding a tin. I stopped. "Come on," he said in mock seriousness. I smiled. Triumphantly, he shouted, "I made you laugh."

He told me that his main objective in life was to make his passing public laugh, saying there was one man who had passed daily for six months resistant to his jokes and cajoling, then one day he had done it, the morose New Yorker had smiled at the latest jocular prodding. My friend had achieved his professional fulfilment.

He occupied about 20 yards of 6th Avenue, most of it outside an Italian restaurant from which he was occasionally fed by the back door. He slept in parks in the summer and in the subway in the winter. If he collected 12 dollars he could get a bath and a shave and wash his clothes at a special centre. By our third meeting, I realised he was a kind, sensitive man of some intelligence whose potential had been destroyed by chance just as my potential had been enhanced by chance. He was living a minimalist life, and to some extent I think he now chose it just as a monk chooses his minimalist life to achieve a special sort of fulfilment not achievable in polyvalent life.

It was to be my birthday the next day. Several of my closest friends were in New York for a scientific conference. Sometimes I think that science and medicine are simply an environment in which we live with the primary function of having relationships with others in a particular and special way. Science is a tool of human relationships. It is an aquarium in which we swim, not to discover the universe, but to discover our inner souls in relation to each other.

My wife and I ate lunch outside the Rockefeller Centre the day before to test the environment. It was ideal: sunshine, an extravagant fountain, minimalism rising to the sky, large prawns in acid vinaigrette, a thousand opaque drops of condensation on the over-cool white wine, all served by the caricature of an over-caring Californian waiter who enjoyed bantering with the jokes that formed the interface between his world and mine. Although a loved woman is the best company for lunch, I looked forward to my birthday with chosen men on the morrow. I ordered five lunches as we had eaten, to be drunk with the same wine. We were to be kings at table.

At noon the next day we met my friends. An Australian, tall, quiet, gentle and innocent with a sense of humour only revealed to those who understood, a man who could play the violin with sensitivity and eat a sackful of oysters in one go. A Dane, a straight, simple man of great loyalty and hard work, who had adopted two small black babies into his blond, blue-eyed family. He loved them with simplicity. A Pole, mystical and passionate who would play Chopin for hours if the vodka bottle was left on the piano. All of them immensely differentiated human beings, totally similar yet totally different. My wife decorated our company and was amused from outside at our small male society.

Lunch is the best of all meals. It is unexpected and carries with it the anticipation of the day. At table the cold and liquid wine made an alchemy of goodwill. I had been given a Zorki camera in Poland. It was a beautiful copy of a Leica made in 1935 (extraordinary that it could have been made with such precision so soon after the Revolution). I had loaded it with colour film, probably for the first time in its life. It was a work of art; I imagined it being used on mountain expeditions in distant lands in a time of flying boats. After lunch we took photographs of each other, guessing the light to demonstrate our primitive photographic skill. After six photographs the camera jammed. It was broken. It had been made in Soviet Russia, taken to Poland, given to me, taken to England, then to New York. It had photographed my birthday, then functioned no more. Its last work was therefore of great value. When developed, the pictures had a soft poetic quality, a fitting end for a noble camera.

Two blocks from the Rockefeller Center was the New York Museum of Modern Art. On the third floor was the painting that I had found the most impressive of any I had ever seen. It was an enormous minimalist canvas by Barnet Newman. I had first seen it thirteen years before when returning from Australia on a languid delicious journey across the Pacific and North America. When I had entered the room which it dominated I had been immediately overwhelmed by its magnificence. My first wife who was with me was not impressed but told me she knew I would find it moving. I had felt instant empathy with its painter. In my mind was a concept without form that was given an exact name when I read the title of the painting. On every visit to New York since then I have visited the Museum of Modern Art.

After more wine and coffee I announced that the ultimate celebration of my birthday would be to visit my favourite painting, which lay only two blocks away. We stood, cheering, the bill was paid with plastic alacrity and we departed in a warm sunlit haze in search of treasure that lay close by. Like a group of happy schoolboys we skipped our way towards discovery. They joked with me about the originality and rare stupidity of such a venture. And then, on the great door of the Museum, "Closed Wednesday afternoon". Oh what conspiracy against us! Oh what worse fate could afflict mankind than to be deprived of art after birthday lunch? A smaller door led into the museum shop. It was open. We entered, by now a hot and random platoon with a frustrated leader on the edge of anger. "Why is the museum closed?"

"Because it is Wednesday."

"That's not possible, it's my birthday."

"I'm sorry it's closed."

"Can I see your superior?"

Then another small grey uninterested administrator chanted the monotone. "I'm sorry it's closed."

"But we have come from Australia, Denmark, Poland, France and England to see one painting, it has to be possible." Again the response was an indifference to real human values.

Hearing this exchange a new man had entered the circle. I knew from his eye that this was the man who would understand. He was active, head to one side, his face alert and enquiring with a smile that told me he liked a challenge. I left the others and addressed him directly. "We are doctors from all over the world who have come here on my birthday to see one painting, please help us." He nodded and disappeared. We, the rabble platoon, looked at each other. They were questioning why they were there. I determined only to accept success. The activist returned, having persuaded higher authority, saying, "OK you've got ten minutes to see one painting. Two guards must go with you." The key to success is the man who understands. Our two guards arrived. There was no mechanism of unlocking the turnstiles on Wednesday afternoon so we all vaulted over, guards included. We then looked at each other in the quiet and deserted hall of the museum, the two guards confused and uncertain how to behave. "Follow me," sez I, starting up the stairs two at a time. (Of course, escalators don't work on Wednesday afternoon.) I knew exactly where it was on the third floor and I knew it would confront us as we entered the room. I gathered us at the top of the last stairs telling the others that we were about to see it. The atmosphere changed from elation at having achieved the impossible to one of quiet anticipation. Hands were dropped, heads slightly bowed. I asked a guard if he could go ahead and light the room. We allowed him a few moments, standing in a subdued light. We moved round a corner and there it was.

It filled the far wall of the plain rectangular room: a long rectangle of brilliant red; as red as carotid blood, its width from horizon to horizon, its height not too great but complementary to its great breadth. On the redness were fine thin vertical lines: one brilliant white, one less white and three of different reds; their spacing, one from another, unmeasurable, unpredicted yet perfect and necessary. As always I was filled with a feeling of nobility and strength, of optimistic power and rightness.

Newman had called his painting *Vir Heroicus Sublimis*. But Newman might not have been the best classical scholar and I suspect he might have meant

Homo Heroicus Sublimis. I find that the use of man (*vir*) as distinct from woman diminishes the picture. To me, it is the essence of the nobility of mankind (*homo*).

We stood about twenty paces from the picture as I explained my feelings about this work. The glow of lunch had dissipated. The guards looked puzzled, the Dane and Australian blank, only one understood: the Pole, he the mystical player of Chopin felt my feeling, he knew that the physical world was simply a substrate which allowed expression of a true reality, that man, the biological, was simply a chalice in which was held man the sublime. The debate opened. "I don't see it," said the Dane. I started the counter-attack and immediately the guards, seeing the argument would have no end, said "time up".

I felt the injustice of deprivation, how could this man ask me to leave the picture that I understood, that was part of my own internal culture? How could he turn off the light and leave this immense and powerful beauty unseen by any human eye, its meaning living and carried within itself, yet unbeheld? For a moment I entered Newman's minimalist anarchy, but then regimental order returned. "Thank you," I said to the guard. We walked through the empty museum. I was elated that we had triumphed on my birthday.

The next afternoon I visited the Frick collection

with the Pole. It was a wonderful display of pictorial art. We played the game of choosing two pictures that we would be allowed to take home. Andrew chose a Dutch interior with layers of light and depths of shadow, and Rembrandt's Polish horseman. His poetic judgement is outstanding, yet bound up with his nationality. (I remember once hearing a singer with him in Cracow, who brought tears to my eyes. He left because the song was in Russian.)

I chose two portraits by Holbein, one of Thomas More, facing left, in green robes, the other Archbishop Cramner, facing right, in similar green robes. More's nobility, honesty and intelligence shone from his face. He was beheaded, and his spirit is an inspiration to me. Cramner's face, with its compromising mediocrity, was set opposite More's for all to see the difference.

The pictorial imagery in the Frick Gallery delighted me, each painting eliciting an emotional response from some corner of my history. But none overwhelmed me as much as Newman' s minimalist abstraction had done. The greater the abstraction in art, the greater it reaches the depths of man, for the depth of man is surely an abstraction.

A Man in Washington

I T HAD the nobility of a capital: open lawns, wide roads and white classical building. Washington itself was not an abstraction, but a series of recognisable human edifices. I stood on a high gallery in the modern art annex of the National Picture Gallery and looked down at a marvel of space and light constructed such that the internal space seemed that it must be much greater than that contained by the outside walls. I looked down onto walkways and galleries the size of aircraft carrier decks, suspended in airy space, angled, one under the other. I was hunting Barnet Newmans. In Cologne I had recognised one from 50 metres. Its blueness had lacked the grandeur of *Vir Heroicus Sublimis*. Already that day in Washington I had seen one in the Gallery. I recognised it as a friend. I stood smiling in front of it, feeling the total abstraction, yet optimism, of its essential vertical lines, knowing that within that picture was a feeling beyond thought.

I went to the information desk and, by chance, found a man who understood. He was a late-middle-aged tall thin academic enthusiast with gold-rimmed glasses.

"Do you have any Barnet Newmans?"

"Yes, we have sixteen, including the stations of the cross, this is the place to come to see Barnet Newman."

I walked slowly with reverent excitement towards the underground rooms. In a corridor on my left I passed one. It was obvious, no need to look, green background with two close yellow vertical lines. The yellow and green merged occasionally in a smudging. It must have been an early one in Newman's development of minimalism. I had not got time to stay. I went on, knowing that ahead of me was treasure.

Through an opening I saw a round room. I entered, and was shocked. The room was polygonal with a canvas on each of fifteen walls. I saw they were very similar canvases but each was different with a dominant feeling of hessian brown, black and white with the expected verticality of focus broken by irregularity. I realised that any picture was not relevant in itself. I had to consider the dynamic whole. I was elated to be completely surrounded by the art of Newman, but I was confused as to its meaning, in contrast to my immediate recognition of *Vir Heroicus Sublimis*.

I sat on the bench in the middle of the room and

slowly rotated myself around so that I looked at each picture in turn. Then I stood and walked the "stations of the cross" from beginning to end, then back to sitting and rotating. In all, I spent about two hours in the room. After my first walk I realised that there were fourteen stations of the cross, the last one followed by a painting that was slightly larger than the rest called *Be II*. It was a white canvas with a thin vertical black line on its extreme right-hand side and a thin warm orange vertical line making the left-hand border of the canvas. It was utterly different in feeling and meaning from the fourteen stations. I could not understand it.

I climbed the marble stairs to the information desk. "Why is an unrelated painting hung after the stations?" I asked.

"I don't know," said the man who understood. "But I'll write to you with an explanation if you give me your address."

I ran back down to the polygonal room to try to understand.

I sat in the middle of the room again and rotated. I saw that from the first to the thirteenth station there was a growing feeling of suffering and approaching death. The fourteenth was a brilliant white canvas with an even more brilliant white left-hand vertical. The death of Christ at the fourteenth station was a white explosion of relief and triumph after the building of suffering from one to thirteen. I went back to the beginning and walked them again. The most striking thing about the first station was the non-symmetrical edge of its right-hand vertical. The contents of the line spilled out of it in jaggedness onto the grey-brown sacking-coloured background. The jaggedness of line recurred in stations three and five and again slightly at twelve. This gave the feeling of an intermittent unresolved problem that interfered with the continuity of the developing concept.

The vertical lines, one or two per canvas, continued from one to nine. They became thicker, on the whole, and more emotive of suffering. White verticals appear from nine to eleven, giving hope of future resolution, but black returns more deeply and widely (but not violently) in twelve and thirteen. This is followed by the total white explosion at fourteen.

I walked round again and felt the build-up of suffering and emotion that was the stations of the cross. I now noted on twelve the vertical had so enlarged as to become the background. However, it was greyish-blue, giving the same total amount of darkness as the thinner black lines on preceding canvases. This allowed an increase in the amount of darkness for thirteen by painting the same area as was grey-blue in twelve completely black in thirteen.

I again returned to walk the stations. The thin

eccentric vertical was on the left from one to six. At seven it became a thicker line, but on the right. This was disturbing, breaking an expected rhythm. The relative complexity of one to four was indicative of emotions in different directions before resolution to a single darkening direction from eight onwards, leading to the glorious resolution of the white fourteenth.

I was taking part in a tragedy as evocative as any by Shakespeare. I felt peace of mind, all passion spent, tired yet refreshed. I then stood in front of *Be II*, immediately after the fourteenth. It was wonderful. Its whiteness contained between thin black and orange lines, each slightly smudged at the interface, had a feeling of optimism. It was complete relief and joy after the journey of the stations. It was a re-statement of the happiness of life. A happiness that I recognised as my life. The stations of the cross were from another life. I again leapt up the stairs to the help desk but there was no man who understood. "Where is the man in the gold-rimmed glasses?" I demanded.

"He's our senior man and can move from place to place as he likes, I don't know where he is," said the substitute.

"Tell him I understand," I said.

"OK," came the non-understanding reply.

.

II

THE WHISTLE BLEW

Cold War in Schleswig-Holstein[4]

"Hello Sunray, this is Starlight"
And the beauty of our names
Mingled in the ether
With the green angles of the ambulance
And its red cross on white
With the muffled clatter of the helicopter
And the chest-thumping pressure of
     distant tank engines
With the purity of wet pine needles
     against my face
And the comforting thickness of the army's
     shirt against my neck

SERGEANT BROWN

For two weeks it had rained upon my tent
In Schleswig-Holstein
And I was officer of the day.
Making my rounds at night
I met Sergeant Brown and his guard
Dripping black in his army cape
And I in mine
Both hooded like wet monks
And I saw the mud in which he stood
Was over the top of his boots
He saluted with his open palm towards me
And the light of my torch
Sparkled in the drops of rain
Hanging from his hand
As I returned his salute sez I:
"How is it George?"
"Magic, Sir, magic," he replied
And the spirit of our brotherhood
Was strengthened by the mud

At a café, after an organ recital
in the Church of St Magnus the Martyr
14th November 1999

1917[5]

The whistle blew
And I rose from the trench
And I carried the cathedral of my soul
Over the parapet
And nothing of me remained upon the
      fire step
And I ascended into thy arms, Oh Lord
Bayonet fixed and nothing in the breach

DENTED

And I put my finger
In the bullet dent
In the brass plate on the door
In the Great Hall of the College of Surgeons
Where Countess Markowitz
Shot out of the window
With her revolver
Across Stephen's Green
And a British Tommy replied
With his Lee-Enfield Mark 1
Leaving the dent of the 303
In the history of Ireland

Royal College of Surgeons, Dublin
25th January 2003

BELFAST

Art thou there, Oh Provo leader
Standing in the dark alone?
Art thou there, Oh British soldier
In thy grey exclusion zone?
While helicopter stands serenely
Covering all its ebb and flow,
Gently waxing, gently waning
Soothing all the earth below.
Oh love each other gentle brothers
In the night of calm and pain
You alone can pierce our future
You alone our end ordain

Belfast
26th March 1988

ZAMARRIPA

Oh the joy you gave
Flying with the cockpit of your Harvard open
Over the Spanish sahara
And your wingman
Cutting a metre from your wing
With his propeller,
And without effect

Brussels

Patagonian Strike

In 1921 the Army
Held the gauchos
With white flag flying
In a shed, that I have seen
And killed them.
So what has changed Argentina?

Buenos Aires

The 2nd Polish Corps

My patient lay in the hospital bed
Unshaven, smelling of urine
And bitten by lice,
Of no fixed abode
Living on the street
And unemployed
Without family or friends.
In his Slavic accent
He declared
"I fought at Monte Cassino"
And my junior doctors in ignorance
Remained unmoved by man or history
And I turned to them
With my hand upon the shoulder
Of my patient
To address them on the greatness
Of the 2nd Polish Corps
And the infinite value
Of all human beings

Barcelona, in a taxi
25th July 2002, 9.40am

Cause and Effect

Hunger begat work
And work begat organisation
And organisation begat power
And power begat plenty
And plenty begat envy
And envy begat war
And war begat work
And work begat organisation
And organisation begat power
And power begat victory
And victory begat justice
And justice begat questioning
And questioning begat reflection
And reflection begat understanding
And understanding begat spirituality
And spirituality begat discussions
And discussions begat war
And war begat hunger

London, in a taxi
16th November 2001

Light in the East

I KNOCKED on the door of the Moscow hotel room. I was filled with anticipation at meeting Gryglewski for the first time, a Pole in Brezhnev's Moscow. In my pocket were a letter and a small vial of white powder I had been asked to deliver to him. He had been difficult to find. I had obtained a list of all the hotels used for foreigners attending the conference but I did not know whether Eastern Bloc scientists would be staying in the same ones as Westerners. It was deep in the time of Brezhnev. All was potentially difficult, all was contorted, relationships were twisted, directions ambiguous. I had started the rounds of the hotels persuading girls at reception to tell me if Professor Gryglewski was staying there (according to my briefing by the Army Special Investigation Branch before I left England, they would all be members of the KGB). Finally, I was standing at his door.

I knocked again and the door opened. There stood a large man with a large Slavic face. (My father, who had served with Poles in the Royal Air Force in the war, had told me you can identify Poles from behind by the massiveness of the outer and lower one-third of their necks.) He grinned, but not with confidence since I saw his mouth was not fully extended.

"I am John Martin, I've brought you a letter from London." (It was later, when I knew him well, that he told me that his immediate thought at that time was "The KGB are really speaking excellent English nowadays".)

He invited me in and we sat in small armchairs with a table between us. He poured me the universal Slavic lubricant and we began to assess each other. I was fairly sure he was Gryglewski, but I was confident in myself in Moscow and I would not have been over-concerned if he were not. He did not know me and mistakes could have been disastrous for a Pole in Moscow. At the last moment, I had replaced a friend in giving a lecture in Moscow. At Moscow airport, when the waiting Minister of Health had realised he had got the stand-in, he immediately dismissed the little girls with bouquets of flowers and I was left to make my own way through security where I had to make a mental reservation when answering "no" to the question "do you have any letters for any person in the Soviet Union?". If caught I would have argued that I thought the question was referring to Soviet citizens, not Poles.

Gryglewski fenced around me probing with his épée.

When I offered him the letter and the tube of white powder he was reluctant and asked me to put it on the table. He was uncertain about me. We discussed our families and our backgrounds. I told him that I had been to a Catholic school, rare for an Englishman. Suddenly, he said "Introibo ad altare Dei". I replied instantly "Ad Deum qui laetificat iuventutem meum". The grin became the smile of a massive extended mouth, he laughed, shook my hand and replaced the vodka with whisky he had reserved. No KGB man would ever know the response at the opening of the Tridentine Mass. The Catholic Pole had identified the Catholic Englishman.

He took the white powder (a rare chemical for his research in Poland) and we parted good friends. I promised to visit him in Cracow. On returning to my hotel I was greeted in the lobby by three Georgian cardiologists I had met earlier each carrying a bottle of Georgian brandy. They were full of friendship and Georgian song as they bore me along towards my room. They were accompanied by two "colleagues" who, when we got to my room, seemed far too beautiful to have been through the rigours of a medical course. I remembered the Army's warning that everyone was in the KGB and felt weak at the prospect at having to face the sergeant of the Special Investigation Branch to confess a breach of military discipline; it would have been worse than going to confession to my uncle.

I avoided the Georgians with the real excuse that I had been invited to a party at the British Embassy. I took a taxi to the beautiful pre-revolution building, which looked across the Moscow river at the Kremlin. Both entrances were blocked with about twenty military police. Damn! I remembered that no-one is allowed into the Embassy by the Russians unless they show a Western passport. Effused with the friendship and the whisky of Gryglewski and the brandy of the Georgians, I had forgotten my passport. I was already late for the party.

I hesitated outside the taxi for less than a second then walked directly to the officer in charge of the party at one of the gates. I stood in front of him and very formally put two fingers of my right hand into the breast pocket of my jacket bringing out my National Westminster Bank credit card. Grasping it by the corner with finger and thumb, I held it up between us.

He immediately saluted, presumably believing this card indicated an emissary from the Queen. I smiled politely and he moved his men to let me pass. Triumphantly, I entered the Embassy grounds with the certain knowledge that we could surely defeat the Soviet military machine if it could be fooled by a credit card.

I had visited Moscow previously in 1975, even deeper in the time of Brezhnev. This was at the invitation of Igor Ivanovich, the worst doctor in the world. He had been allowed to come to England for six months since his father was a senior and influential surgeon in Moscow. Igor slept in the next room to mine in the Children's Hospital. His Russian medical training had not quite prepared him for working as a doctor in England. My phone would ring in the night. A heavy Russian accent would ask: "John, I am in Casualty with a patient who is fitting, what do I do?"

"Give diazepam."

"Thank you."

Back to sleep; then two minutes later on the phone again. "John, how do I give diazepam?"

"You ask the nurse to draw up 5mg into a syringe and you give it slowly into a vein."

"Thank you, John."

Igor loved England. His delight was to eat fish and chips while watching a cowboy film on television. The rest of us living in the hospital had to support him by buying him beer and other essentials of life since his income was so low. He was paid as an English doctor for his six months' stay but he had to pay his wages to the Soviet Embassy in London, who returned what he would have got in Moscow: two or three pounds a week.

Igor became more downcast as his time for leaving approached. Then he made a wonderful discovery. The Soviet Embassy had not heard of the tax rebate.

Since he had only worked for six months, but had paid full tax, on leaving he would be given back several hundred pounds overpaid tax. This would be a king's ransom in Moscow. He received a form to claim the money, still uncertain how to get it to Moscow until he saw a section on the bottom: "Do you wish to pay the tax rebate to a third Party?" Yes, I agreed to receive the cash and bring it to Moscow.

Five weeks later there I was at Moscow Airport with Igor's cash in my pocket, undeclared on my foreign currency declaration form. I was sure that if I was caught I could give a convincing excuse: I was of extremely low intelligence and did not understand the form properly, or my special type of cataracts stopped me from reading the obscure print on the cheap grey paper. My confidence carried me through, plus the fact that the man behind me dropped a bottle of whisky, which broke on the floor. The golden liquid immediately focused the attention of all police present.

I stayed in a small hotel where I was contacted by Igor and asked to come to his flat for dinner. His flat was two small rooms where he lived with his wife. She had taken the day off her job in the film industry to cook our dinner. She stayed in the other room (the kitchen) while we two men ate a succession of courses that she brought us. After each course Igor retrieved a bottle of vodka from the January snow on the windowsill, refilling my glass. The vodka was so cold that it outlined my oesophagus, stomach and first part of the duodenum as though they were frozen glass. Until this time, our comments on politics had been neutral. Now full of good food and vodka, Igor took up his guitar to play me "Beautiful Black Eyes", "the favourite song of a White Russian General". His eyes twinkled as he sang with passion. Then we spoke about real things.

His grandfather had been a Pole who had taken part in the October Revolution. He told me of the horrors of Stalin's Moscow and the difficulties of his father who was a Professor but not a party member.

The next day I visited one of Moscow's Children's hospitals with Igor and his father the surgeon. I wore a long wrap-around white coat and a white hat. I felt like Dr Zhivago as I knelt by the bed of a child to examine his abdomen. He was the son of the Italian Ambassador who had suspected appendicitis. The old Professor was uncertain whether to operate or not and I believe that he thought that the hand of a Western doctor might provide some reassurance in his difficult geo-political decision.

Before returning to England I spent a few days in Leningrad. My train journey to Leningrad was a rare wonder. Snow was piled high beside the track and beyond January darkness. Old ladies served tea from samovars at the end of the carriage. In the restaurant car the menu was hand-written in Cyrillic script. A group of good-humoured soldiers helped by miming the whole menu for me. It began with fish soup, which was explained by one of them swimming in mid-air while another poured water into a bowl. The restaurant car was a warm golden shelter of humanity speeding through the January snow.

In Leningrad I had stayed at the Finland Station Hotel. This allowed me to walk on foot and travel back to the hotel by tram. The first letter of "Finland" in Russian in a phi (Ø) which I could easily recognise on the destination board of my tram. I remember one day in a crowded tram being jammed against a window and in my belly was the small punch attached to the tram's wall that good citizens would use to invalidate their tickets. I was tapped on the shoulder by a citizen who ostentatiously proffered his ticket to me for punching "spasibo" ("please"). I punched it, giving back to him with "pojalsta" ("don't mention it"), one of my ten words in Russian. I then became the centre of attention with all offering me their tickets like good citizens should: there was a constant chorus of "spasiba" followed by my "pojalsta"— oh what joy to be accepted as a comrade!

One of the most restrained beauties I have seen was the vision of the fortress of St Peter and St Paul on its island in the Neva River. Moscow had been a Russian city, but Leningrad was a truly European city. On the January afternoon the sky was grey, the massive walls of the fortress were grey, the elegant towers of the cathedral were grey and the heaped-up massive blocks of ice on the Neva were grey. But there in the midst was a thin tall spire of shining gold, spectacular and precious as the single colour, and that of gold, in the grey monotone.

As I left the bridge over the Neva I passed an alleyway at the end of which was a courtyard. I caught a glimpse of a coffin without a lid with a body, slightly raised above the edges of the coffin, looking towards heaven. Men and women knelt in an arc around it. A black-robed man in a tall hat stood within the arc. Then the glimpse was gone. There was more to Russia than cold vodka and Socialist realism. Other strata were in the structure. Which of them would be dissolved by the solvent of time and which would remain was not then clear.

However, matters in the East were becoming clearer by the time I fulfilled the promise given to Gryglewski in Moscow that I should visit him in Cracow. We had arranged by letter that I should give a lecture in the Academy of Medicine in the third week of December 1981, and that I should spend some time discussing research. The date was fixed; I had my visa and arranged my plane tickets. Then, two days before I was due to leave, martial law was declared. There was no telephone or post communication with Poland. Many flights were cancelled. The pro-solidarity embassy in London was uncertain what to advise me to do, however they said that the safest thing was not to go. But how could I not go because there were difficulties in Poland? In any case, surely it would be interesting to see what was martial law. I turned up for my flight and it left. I arrived in Warsaw, and after a vigorous personal search, I got the plane to Cracow. Throughout the journey militiamen stood in the aisle of the plane, wearing crash helmets and holding truncheons. I could not conceal my mirth when I realised that to use the toilet one had to raise one's hand, then be escorted by a behelmeted policeman who stood behind one, door open, till the completion of the process.

I arrived at the small Cracow airport whose buildings seemed as though they might belong to a gliding club in Yorkshire. The few people on the plane quickly cleared and I was left standing outside the tiny huts of the airport on a small country road surrounded by trees. There was no-one; no bus, taxi, bicycle or dog. I went back into the airport to ask how I could telephone Gryglewski. I was told that no telephones were working in Poland because of martial law. That is why I had not been able to tell Gryglewski that I was coming and when I would arrive. I asked which way was Cracow, "Turn left". I turned left, and walked down the country road. It was good luck that I always travelled light.

After ten minutes a car approached, a small Polish Fiat 650. I put up my hand to wave; an ambiguous signal since I did not want to be perceived as asking for a lift. The car stopped, a middle-aged man looked at me through the open window. "Anglia," ("England") I said, one of my five words of Polish. I was met by a torrent of Polish, a great smile and an open door. I showed him the address of Gryglewski but he was clearly hesitant about taking me to an address, or he didn't know where it was. We drove into Cracow, which was a continuum of beautiful Renaissance buildings, but all sad, covered by a grey grime. No human presence in the streets relieved the darkness. He dropped me on a corner of the main square. It was massive and flat, elegant and poetic in a mixture of styles of architecture. In one corner was the beautiful asymmetric brick mediaeval cathedral and in the middle of the square a great low colonnaded hall. And still all was drab and grey with the wall beside me crumbling.

There were four or five darkly clad figures crossing the square and half-a-dozen military vehicles, mostly armoured personnel carriers. I walked up to the nearest which had two men sitting on top. The grey paint of the vehicle and their ugly grey communist uniforms added to the air of gloom in the square. "Anglia," again I introduced myself. I showed one of them Gryglewski's address typed on a piece of paper. He was not friendly but pointed across the square to three cars that I recognised as taxis. I walked across the unswept greyness, not that there was litter (that would have been removed by good comrades) but there lay grey silt of oppression that had not been evaporated by human happiness.

The sadness of the place was palpable. I opened the door of the first taxi. I showed him the paper and a five pound note (I had not been able to change money) and we were off. Five minutes later I stood outside a small block of flats with the taxi driver pointing me up the stairs. I found Gryglewski's number and for the second time in my life I knocked on his door not knowing what to expect. The door opened.

Gryglewski stood there for a moment without moving. Then filled with delight at the unexpected, he welcomed me warmly. He led me into the warm glow of his flat where I drank vodka with cherries in it. He and his wife explained that because of martial law there were no telephones in operation and little food. Certainly, they had not expected me to come from the West.

I was determined to try to carry on as normal and the next day I gave my lecture in the Copernicus Medical Academy. I did not truly grasp the significance to students of that lecture until I was in Cracow 13 years later, when I was thanked for the lecture by doctors who had been students at the time. "We said you were the light from the West," said one.

The Poles were generous in their difficulties. Even though there was very little petrol, they collected enough together, several people giving donations, to send me to see the Tatra Mountains on the borders of Czechoslovakia. A young doctor drove me there along deserted roads, past long thin fields where horses pulled ploughs. (At least lack of economic development in Eastern Europe had preserved some things of beauty that had been lost in the West). She took me to a lake called "The Eye of the Sea" where the water was transparent to its depths.

We decided to walk further into the hills. She told me about Solidarity, about the Polish Pope who had once been the students' chaplain in Cracow. She was warm, honest, strong and determined to resist injustice. We walked up a long steep path. The mountain ahead of us was covered in cloud. Once it cleared to reveal perpendicular long jagged teeth that must have capped the mountain we were skirting. It rained incessantly as we climbed into the cloud. She, wearing a bright yellow oilskin jacket, I my brown Barbour. We came to a rim of stone and grass above us over whose lip spilled a torrent of water. The rim ran left and right above us like the edge of a thin cup. I realised with excitement that a body of water must be held by the rim. It must have been terminal moraine with a glacial tarn behind it. I raced the last few yards to get my head over the rim. There at the level of my eyes was a flat sheet of black water and beyond it the grey scree of a mountain falling almost vertically into the tarn. The clouds cleared immediately as I climbed over the rim, revealing vertical grey rock above the scree, so high I had to bend my head back to see the peak. It was Rysy, the highest mountain in Poland. Its peak was the border with Czechoslovakia.

We walked around the tarn on dark pebbles towards a boulder the size of a small house. Its shape on top was strangely elongated. As I approached I realised that the protrusions on top of the boulder were two border guards. Their long grey cloaks ran smoothly from the hoods over their heads almost to their ankles. The greyness of them was at one with the greyness of the boulder on which they stood motionless. Both they and the boulder dripped with rain. Behind them grey scree in the distance.

"Can we talk to them?" sez I.

"No, absolutely not, never speak to the military." I was shocked by her commitment contrasting with my naïve intrusion. She was governing her human destiny from her own will in a way that I did not have the opportunity to do. She stood out in her yellow jacket against the monotone dark rocks and uniforms of the guards: golden in the grey.

Many years later in a free and independent Poland, I made great friends with one who had been skiing in the same area of the Tatras two months after I was there. She told me that she had gone skiing alone to escape the miseries of martial law. It was not possible to organise companions because there were still no telephones working and permission was needed to travel. The slope above Zakopane was almost deserted, but in the first afternoon she had met three other friends who had had the same idea: to ski alone to forget totalitarianism.

At the end of the afternoon they had ended up by the car of one of them, at the bottom of the mountain. They were overjoyed to have met each other. In the car was a cassette recorder. They opened the door of the car so that its yellow light lit the snow beside it. In that pool of golden light they danced on the snow to a tape of "Hotel California". Their intoxicated happiness was self-sustaining. A police car arrived and stopped 20 to 30 metres away. The policemen got out, stood by their car watching the scene. The dancing and laughing continued. The policemen did not approach, as if the human fellowship itself had the power to repel them.

This year I have sat in the market place in Cracow,

the same market place where I asked the soldier on the armoured personnel carrier for directions. The world had become transformed. I drank a beer under an umbrella at a table on the pavement. I was surrounded by laughing Poles dressed in every mode from formal to riotous informality and non-conformity. There must have been a thousand people in the square laughing, chattering, disputing and, in one corner, dancing. Music was everywhere — a peasant band from the hills, a rock guitarist, two Russians singing sadly. Sunlight flooded all.

I thought back to my visits to the East over the past eighteen years. I remembered all those small shelters of human warmth and nobility that I had encountered. The cold vodka meal in the flat in Moscow, the friendship of the Russian soldiers in the warm restaurant car of the Leningrad train, the golden spire of the Cathedral of St Peter and St Paul, Gryglewski's home in Cracow, my friend dancing on the snow to "Hotel California", and the young doctor in her yellow oilskin. The points of golden warmth had grown and coalesced and overflowed, banishing the grey and flooding the market square of Cracow.

WATCHMAN

IN 1979 I volunteered to go to Hong Kong for two months as a medical officer with the Ghurka Field Force in the New Territories. The main job of the army was to catch illegal immigrants ("IIs") who had come over the border from China and to send them back. The job was not popular among the soldiers on the ground or the helicopter pilots in the air. Some British soldiers would load their pockets with chocolate to give to the poor "IIs" when caught. Occasionally, a blind eye was turned to their escape. However, the immensely loyal Ghurkas, as always, relished their duty.

One night I was "Watchman, New Territories". This was a duty that rotated among all junior officers. The watchman and his sergeant slept in the head-quarters and had to deal with any military problems that arose in the colonial territories on the Chinese mainland. I went to sleep on the watchman's bed wearing my green tropical combat uniform, feeling apprehensive yet exhilarated in my role for a night.

I was in command of one of the last corners of the British Empire.

In the early hours of the morning, Sergeant Beswick woke me: "There's something going on, Sir, you'd better come". A Ghurka sergeant was in the entrance to HQ. His salute and "attention" were performed with the energy and total commitment of all Ghurka soldiers. With his little English he told me that his patrol had come across a group of "IIs" in the night near the border with the People's Republic of China. When challenged the Chinese had run away. The Ghurkas had pursued them until they came to a cliff over which the Chinese had fallen in the dark. He led me outside. In the courtyard there was a line of Land-Rovers. In the back of the first there were two men who looked as though they might have broken limbs, in the second a man with cuts to his face and another who moaned with pain and who appeared to have a broken lower jaw. They all wore the typical Chinese communist black pyjamas. All was seen in the light of the Ghurka sergeant's torch. I asked for the fifteen or so Chinese to be taken out of the Land-Rovers and into the medical centre where I would see them, reverting to my role of medical officer.

In the meantime, I considered what to do. There was only a small doubt about the reported incident in my mind until Sergeant Beswick said, "Do you think they done 'em over, Sir?" He had said what I didn't want to think: could these good, simple, loyal Ghurkas have assaulted the Chinese and fabricated the story of them falling over the cliff? I was the Watchman. I could accept the story and that would be the end of the matter. However, I represented authority this night in this last remnant of the British Empire. I felt strong and elated knowing what I should do. I had to discover the truth and make sure justice was done to the Chinese if they had been beaten and that the truth was disseminated if the Ghurkas' story were true.

I first spoke to the Ghurka sergeant again, then to two corporals, one of whom spoke English well. They all said that the "IIs" had been chased in the night and they had fallen over a cliff. Each one was adamant. Before going to the medical centre I asked Sergeant Beswick to find interpreters who would speak the same Cantonese dialect as the prisoners (or patients as I was about to think of them). He was to wake up cooks and drivers until we had someone who could communicate with the "IIs".

In the medical centre I examined the Chinese communist peasants who were prepared to risk much to get to Hong Kong. The first half dozen I examined all had injuries that could have been caused by falling over a cliff or having been beaten with a rifle. The interpreters arrived sleepy and disgruntled. One clearly communicated well with the injured who I was able to interview one by one, each in isolation from the rest.

After four conversations it was clear they all told the same story, even in detail: they came across the border about ten o'clock at night having been brought under the wire by a guide to whom they had paid money. He had left them at a rocky place about half and hour's walk from the border saying he would return later. While hiding there they had been surprised by soldiers. They were very frightened and they ran into the darkness. After a short distance of running and stumbling they had fallen over a cliff onto stones below. Some of the group must have got up and continued fleeing. Those who I saw were injured and could not move. The Ghurka patrol was quickly upon them having come down the cliff. The Ghurkas had treated them with kindness, carrying them to their vehicles. My thought that injustice might have been done was justified from the nature of the injuries. However, I was now sure that the Ghurkas had behaved well.

Even the innocent must be prepared to receive accusations of wrongdoing if there is to be a system of justice. Sergeant Beswick came in saying that the patrol's platoon commander was on the telephone and wanted to speak to the Watchman. He was an

English lieutenant who had heard on the radio from his sergeant that he had brought in injured Chinese. He was very concerned that his men might have misbehaved. I was able to tell him that I had enquired as fully as was necessary and that I believed no crime had been committed and, in fact, the Chinese reported that the Ghurkas had behaved with kindness. He was much relieved when I, as Watchman, told him nothing more need be done in the matter.

But the best of the story is yet to come. The most severely injured man was the one with the fractured lower jaw. I had previously seen that his breathing was safe and I now returned to him, reverting once more from Watchman to doctor. He could speak only indistinctly with difficulty out of the corner of his mouth. When I sat on his bed he threw his arms round my neck and would not let go, crying out in Cantonese. The interpreter told me that he said that I was the first European that he had even seen and that he knew that he could trust me. He pleaded repeatedly for me not to send him back to China.

At that time there was a law that all illegal immigrants from China should be sent back. But if an "II" succeeded in reaching Hong Kong island itself, he was allowed to stay and given a Hong Kong passport. This was to stop the exploitation of vulnerable

"IIs" without papers in Hong Kong by the resident Hong Kong Chinese. Such a law had stopped many a poor "II" living in slavery with deportation being the only consequence of them asking for help.

The other injured prisoners could be treated in the New Territories. It occurred to me that if I decided this man needed specialist maxillofacial surgical treatment in Hong Kong then to send him there would be to send him to the freedom he desired. I therefore called an ambulance, wrote a referring letter and sent him with a medical orderly escort to a hospital on Hong Kong island. He left me confused and unhappy, not knowing the consequences of the journey on which I had sent him.

Avignon
11th July 1994

III

THE BRIDGE AT REGENSBURG

INTIMACY I

And I smiled at him
Because he was smiling at them
Because they smiled at each other
And I carried away their smile

Beside the Thames
11th July 2003

TRODDEN

In Borough Market
An apple dropped from my bag
And ran alone along the ground
And a man, seeing it running past his foot
Without thought
Of whence it came or whither it went
Trod on it to crush it
Why did you do that? sez I
And he not knowing invented a defence
Not knowing his trodden destruction
Began a million years ago
And when he left
I watched the crushed apple
Lose entropy before my eyes
As others walked upon its parts
Distributing its disorder upon the road

28th February 2003

Justice, Truth and Goodness[6]

And I thought Aquinas great
Until Anselm
Came alone
Out of the darkness,
Walking barefoot on the stones of Canterbury
Carrying the candle of his soul
Into the cranium of his mind

Paris to Cracow
22nd May 1994

ARROW[7]

Whither flyest thee my arrow?
Through what infinite swoon
What infinite progression
What infinite extrapolation
Through what infinite function
Do you curve?
The nature of thy flight
Is to be indivisible

En route to Bermuda
2nd May 1990

A Syllogism

Why do I marvel at the similarity
Of the branching of the lungs
To the naked structure of the tree in winter?
They could not be otherwise
Since they both seek oxygen.
I wonder at the laws of physics
Because I am from another world

I have climbed over a monastery wall only twice (that is from the outside). Once in Greece and once in Øm in Jutland where I met Abbot Jens. His skeleton was lying on gravel. He was a big man with his left humerus slightly shorter than his right. The left humerus bore a large callus, the sign of a healed fracture, that had been received in the thirteenth century when German bandits had raided the monastery for horses. As I looked at his wound, the deterministic Marxist theory of history came into my mind. I was seeing the actual healed wound caused over 700 years before and it was moving me.

ABBOT JENS
ABBOT OF ØM, KLOSTER, JUTLAND
1246-1249

Today I looked into the face of the dead monk
Smitten by the German warrior
Robbing his monastery of horses.
I saw the healed wound in his arm:
The history of a moment
Determining him
Determining me
Determining this
Determining you

Aarhus

SUFFERING

I held him within my arms
And the child-man wept
And I wept within my heart
I cleaned his teeth
And cut his nails
And saw the son I never knew
Was here, within my arms
Dying from a lack of God within the world
Dying because the comet did not return
But left its orb and flew into eternal darkness

Macclesfield
28th March 1994

ALEXI

The child skated across the ice,
With grace
Yet walking on the snow fell upon
His face
The hole in his brain extended
To the visual cortex on the left
Yet with his right hand he was deft,
He stood at the piano
And sang to me with joy,
He was complete, a total human boy

Aarhus – London
8th January 1996

HAYDN[8]

In this quartet lies the nature of man
All is in the relationship
Nothing in the note
Duns Scotus is vindicated
The modality is unquestionable
Event is the cause not the effect
In the note lies the triviality of my science
A science which attaches the key to the hammer,
In the relationship lies life infinite

ANALYSIS

Then men were press-ganged
By a bunch of Navy thugs
Taken from the inn
To live without happiness
To serve a constricted life
Of intense activity
But their human potential
Denied

Now we are press-ganged
By the deformities
Of our own evolution
To be constricted
With the same result

The sailors knew the cause
And understood their fate
We do not

In flight Singapore to London
27th November 2003

The Soul in Evolution[9]

DOES EVOLUTION contain all we are, and did God design it? If God exists as the cause of a creation then he certainly did. If matter existed for ever, even if "for ever" is in a curve, then he did not. If a soul exists, then did it also evolve, did it recapitulate evolution in the development of man, and does it similarly evolve within an individual? Is the spirit of man fixed or does it change?

There is evidence that evolution has not progressed with increments in development matching increments in time. It has proceeded in pulses followed by pauses. Platelets are tiny cells in the blood that are absolutely necessary for the coagulation of the blood. If they were absent then one would bleed to death in one form or another. They are found in all mammals from the smallest mouse to the whale, and of course including man. Down the microscope they are almost identical in all mammals apart from their size (smaller animals having smaller platelets and bigger ones bigger). Their function in all species is identical: to stop bleeding. But other orders (like birds and reptiles) have the same problem of inhibiting bleeding but do not have platelets. The reason why mammals have platelets remains a mystery. However, they are a mark of a mammal. When pre-mammals became mammals they continued with arms, legs and nostrils from before, yet in one great jump they created platelets to respond to a unique and novel need which remains unknown. Evolution had jumped. Does the spirit also jump?

After spending three and a half years studying in Spain, in the time of Franco, I returned by train to modern Europe. The National Museum of Polychromatic Art in Valladolid was an expression of Spanish Catholicism that had proceeded without challenge of reformation. Intense and over-gorgeous statues showed every detail of the body with a salient feature picked out in exaggerated colour. I had left Spain where my advance had been intellectual; as the train covered France I knew that unknown wonder lay ahead. A wonder that would be more than intellectual.

I stayed with my Aunt Alice in rue Chardon Lagache, a street name I repeated to myself to emphasise its soft Frenchness after years of harsher Spanish names. She cooked dinner, which included spinach pounded with garlic into its essence. We passed an evening talking of her life in the French cantonment in Shanghai and later as an English woman in German Paris where she would play the indignant French woman when German officers approached her. Next morning I walked through Paris and by chance found the Museum of Modern Art, in the Palace de Tokyo near the Trocadéro. It is an open, white, symmetrical building which might have been austere, like a Spanish arch is austere, but it was, and is, not. It is constructed with fulfilling purity, full of light without a shaft of light to be seen.

I entered and walked through an abstract hall that contained nothing that prepared me for one of the greatest experiences of my life. I climbed steps that were flat and wide and white. I entered an upper room, again wide, tall, simple, and full of light. And there it was in front of me, a painting, square and big. It was a white background with three of four great thick, black brush strokes, each as wide as two out-stretched hands, each stroke ragged at its beginning and end. It overwhelmed me. Its deep and direct humanity travelled to my soul, without me intervening. I had no training, no education, and no experience in abstract art, and here it was overwhelming me with a feeling of depth, distance, and greatness; a contact that moved me as I had never been moved before. I felt a part of me that I had not felt before. I learned that there were depths within my spirit, which in a moment could be understood without effort, as easily as a bird swoops from a high cliff.

The painting was by Franz Kline who I learned was an American minimalist artist. In painting it he had in some way analysed himself. There in the Palais de Tokyo I was receiving a second analysis. The painting was utterly abstract, making me realise that what I could experience from it was without limit. I stood for a long, long time, not in glory but in deep contented strength.

There were three other paintings by Kline, each with great black strokes on white. Each one elicited a slightly different feeling, but from within the same part of my soul. I was a new man, but I sensed not my last man.

I was now late for lunch with my Aunt. I stopped a taxi in Avenue President Wilson and got in the back seat. The driver was a young woman, something unthinkable in Spain. She drove with energy and courage.

"Vous conduisez comme le diable," I said.

She turned her head, saying: "Je suis le diable."

Yes, polychromatic art was behind me and more than abstraction was ahead.

I had undergone a similar leap earlier while study-ing philosophy in Spain, which was a mixture of an intellectual and spiritual advance. Thomas Aquinas had become my hero. Based upon Aristotle he had constructed a formalised system of analysing the observed world, which gave rise to a way of organising human society based upon evidence, evidence gained by scientific method as equally scientific as the methodology of physics, or biology.

This methodology had been extended to a proof of the existence of God by an analysis of cause and effect. But a proof wonderfully tempered by Aristotle's principle of moral certainty. This states that the quality of certainty that can be achieved in philosophy is such that one has to recognise the possibility of the opposite being true; however, in a world where action is needed it is more reasonable to act in the direction argued. This was a wonderful, precise, intellectually analytical view of the world. I read it, wrote it, argued it, and liked it.

Then I read Anselm and a depth of charge occurred similar to the one which happened when I saw Franz Kline's painting in Paris. Anselm was made Archbishop of Canterbury in 1093. He was an Italian, educated in Normandy. In his book *Monologion* he made an important transition from analysis to poetic insight. He wrote before Aquinas but I read him after Aquinas, and that is the right way to do it. He said some wonderful things like "omne peccatum est iniustitia" which arises from an understanding of the nature of man and the nature of society which echoed Augustine. But what moved me was his proof of the existence of God. It is very simple and direct and you either see its meaning or not. There is no half measure, no slow approach building up arguments as with Aquinas. There it is. You see it or you don't. The vision is not from intellectual analysis but from insight.

I was nineteen years old when I read "If goodness, truth and justice exist then God cannot not exist". I had immediate insight into its meaning and consequences. I dived into a pool of infinite depth. I knew what Anselm knew, not by analysis, but just by knowing. I also felt a different part of me was involved in the knowing from that part which knew what Aquinas knew.

I returned to Anselm's proof again in my twenties. But this time I read it with no insight. I had lost the ability to see. This concerned me but repeated trying brought no insight. Then in my forties, when Anselm was long forgotten, I found a book by Southern on Anselm. I opened it, read the proof and there it was, I saw it again. Insight had returned. The same knowledge and feeling of infinite depth that I had known at the age of nineteen in northern Spain had returned in a bookshop in London.

Another comparison of myself over time occurred in the mosque in Córdoba, again by chance. When I was fifty I looked forward to seeing the hundreds of red mozarabic arches that held the roof of what was once the biggest mosque in the world, when Al-Andaluz was the glory of the world.

At the back of the mosque, set high in the wall are four Moorish windows, small and regular, but glazed with glass of wonderful ancient colour: blue, red, green and yellow, all colours of Arabic meaning. Each colour was only used once in a block, and its edges were linear yet placed irregularly in relation to the others. The summer sun of Spain smeared colour on the floor of the mosque.

In the moment of perceiving and being moved by this beauty I remembered that I had stood in the same place in my youth and seen the same sun through the same coloured glass. I saw myself wearing the khaki shirt and shorts. I even remembered the packet of Bisonte cigarettes in my breast pocket. And I knew the feeling that I had felt when I was nineteen, which came to me without recall. And it was the same feeling that I had today. I was the same man with the same soul. But within that moment I felt more than the original feeling, not a modification of the joy of beauty but something more besides, the consequences of having seen a thousand suns between the first and

second viewing of these windows, and a modulation
of the happiness by an understanding of time.

Granada
July 2003

THE BRIDGE AT REGENSBURG

S TANDING on the bridge at Regensburg, I felt the power of the first structure on the Danube that inhibited navigation from the Black Sea. Kneeling in the Cathedral I was moved by its beauty; men achieving a great structure, not to fulfil their biology, but to make something that is more than their molecules.

While my friends argue over how blood cells stick to arteries, I am here contacted by the medieval man who contrived the ecstatic restraint of pale, shallow water green and grey windows high in the Cathedral. I begin to see the solution. The biology of the body and the physics of the world are destined to support something different from their concrete substance. Something within which there is real life.

Duns Scotus understood. Does the relationship between two objects have existence in itself? When an eagle stands upon a branch it has a relationship in space with the tree. When it has flown the relationship still exists. The water in the Danube will carry the history of every contact with the bank from Regensburg to the Black Sea. It will be changed by a million homeopathic contacts. But those are simple, obvious, measurable physical changes. When the water has passed, does the relationship it had with the bridge still exist?

Bavaria was full of beauty. There were clocks everywhere, often on towers with proportions that pleased me. Clocks with dials of blue and numbers of red. Hands with fingers of gold counter-balanced by warm round bulging golden female weights. The Bavarian clock-makers had realised that to measure time was necessary, to measure it beautifully was human. Is the desire for beauty something that exists independently of man, the collection of organs and cells? When I watch the autopsy of my patient I find nothing that desires beauty. I see what drove him to eat, therefore to farm, therefore to organise markets. I see what drove him to reproduce, desire sex, make rules about behaviour. Yet I see nothing that needs beauty.

Is not beauty something we seek that has existence outside our bodies? A thing that exists like the relationship of the water to the bridge or the eagle to the tree. Is there a reality outside my biology? I explore how cells stick to arteries, I take apart their insides, discover the insides of their insides until I know the atoms of the molecules that make the cells stick. But where is man desiring beauty?

Regensburg, 1992

IV

BOSPHORUS

I lunched with my wife in a restaurant separated from the Bosphorus by only a narrow road. It was on the right bank halfway between Istanbul and the Black Sea. Our table was by the window so that we were only yards from the water. I looked up to see a ship beside us. It was moving silently downstream only a few feet from the shore in what must have been the deep channel. Its grey-green side was so enormous that it filled all my vision and I had to look upwards out of the window to see the top of its side. It was dramatically enormous. Its silence was primeval, its closeness amazing. After lunch we slept.

BOSPHORUS

Mighty is the ship upon the Bosphorus
And precious is your sleep beside me.

Istanbul
1989

MAJ DU SØDE[10]

I fried asparagus in hot oil
And watched her teeth
Penetrate the brown crispness
To find the taste within
And then we saw the beauty
Of the clam shells
Restrained grey and white
Each unique while washed
With sunlight splashed water
Then I watched each open clam
Enter her mouth
As she took the flesh
With teeth and tongue
And white burgundy
In my mouth
Tasting of her inner depth and complexity
With subtle gentle northern light
And then I stood

And in her farewell
She did touch her breast
Against my arm

Whilst listening to Brahms
Church of St Agnes and St Ann
London
6th May 2003, 1.45pm

CLOSE DISTANCE

She travelling from Berlin to Lübeck
In the rain, in the night, driving fast
And I warm and safe before the fire in London
And I telephoned her and we spoke
I heard the rhythm of the windscreen wiper
      on glass
And the rain beating on the roof above her head
I imagined the blue of her eyes in the yellow
      dashboard light
And the blond of her hair upon her cheek

We spoke of that moment as if we were together
Of a hot bath and a glass of wine
And cooking duck and tender kisses
We made a thing between us that lasted
A reality that belonged to us
And if she had died at that moment
On the North German plain
It would continue to exist

London
9th March 2003

Girl Begging in a Bar

She bedraggled, wet in the night, degenerate
Small, innocent, wounded young, near the
        end and lost
And I full, strong, dry, rich; but lost
And I placed the fresh new notes
Into her hand without my eyes looking
        into hers
And I left into the darkness.
Hours later, at great and unknown distance
The bond between us grew
With its own strength
In the dark, in the night
Neither she nor I knowing our destiny,
But the bond grew

Seville
26th January 2000

Standing in a bar in Seville three law students were drinking red wine, they wore the black cloaks of a "tuna": a student band of singers and players. At some distance a young man stood drinking a glass of wine with a young woman. He went and spoke to the tuna and returned to his wine. Having finished their glasses the tuna surrounded the girl and the young man stood apart. They sang to her of her beauty and bearing. She stood silently as tears appeared in her eyes and ran down her cheeks. The band ended with a flourish and left into the street, playing a new song to which they ran dancing along the road. She was changed.

THE TUNA

In the light from the bar
The tuna sang to the girl,
Five men in truth and honesty
And that truth flowed in the wetness
    of her tears
And when they left the truth stayed

Seville
26th January 2000

Dr Soumie Park's father is a Korean consul in Vladivostok. Her piano is there marooned.

VLADIVOSTOK

Her piano in Vladivostok lay
And she to me did say
That snow would melt
When she would play

London
21st December 1994

TIME AND THE TRAIN

The whistle blew
I held her hand
And still there was a massive time
And the train moved a centimetre
And I kissed her lips
And still I was with her
And the kiss ended
I moved with her hands held
And the time was profound
And its length long
I quickened my pace beside the train,
Holding her hand
And she was with me
And I saw how slowly the tear in her
      eye began to form
And again I began to move towards her
My hand clasping her shoulder
She grasped my collar
And life was being lived

The sun was setting and rising
And I began to take my next breath
With new understanding
And she was gone

Sheffield
16th April 1994

NEW ENGLAND

All calm all clear
All New England flat and placid water
And then, perceived, woman dog and boat
    as one
But they were hers
I standing at the point of the arc described by
    her rudder
And she smiled
And upturned her eyes of ashen green
A single drop of water fell from a rope
On to the surface of the flat and limpid pond
And she saw it
While the sea poured through Woods Hole
    Sound

Cape Cod
19th May 2002

YOU ARE

You are the pull of the deep unknown fish
     on my line
In the cool sunshine after dawn when the tide
     is about to run
And the rock is golden

You are the silent curve of the wave
The instant before it breaks.

You are the pistol in my hand
With my finger at first pressure, for ever

You are the first smell of eucalyptus
From the leaf crushed by my boot

NOCTE

Flying from the Isle de France
And racing across Burgundy
At one hundred miles an hour
With my loved woman curled
Asleep on the back seat
Warm under blanket
In the night, in the dark
Headlights scattered in falling snow
Mind clear vision intense
Love pure and protecting
Ahead the Alps which I will cross
With her sleeping behind me

London
26th November 2001

LOVE

Why do I love thee?
Because what is between thee and me
Is an analogy for what is
Between God and me
And God and thee
Amen

London
11th February 2002

BONN

And I have conquered all
Save you my love
And the curve of thee
Is the death of me
My love

Bonn
6th October 1993

INTIMACY II

I am as close to you
As a bullet in the breach
Locked in oiled gun metal

London 1990

WOMAN OF MY LIFE

Oh thou woman of my life
How thou shouldst have been my wife
But I poor fool did lose thee
Because I could not bring myself to be
A man who knew me

My Child

Where is my child
Is she never
Or is she in the stars of heaven
Forever?

Paris
March 1994

USTED[11]

In the sun reflected from the Arab wall
She addressed me as a Horseman
And the dignity of the title
Clasped us
The darkness of her eyes and skin
And the beauty of her nose
Showed the genes of Arab and Visigoth
Had ridden through time to me
The dignity of the word
And the beauty of the gene mixed
As we deferred our contact
By referring to each other
As another

Granada
24th July 2003, 11.00pm

SUFFOLK '93

I saw three earth-brown deer
On the flat dark land
Run before me

And I drank a pint
Of red-brown beer
In front of the fire
That warmed me

Suffolk
1993

AN AMERICAN

And he the idiot castrated himself
Upon the knife of his own stupidity
Dying for trivia without
When within was infinity

On hearing an American
prattling in "The Three Little Pigs"

ROLAND

Roland was a nasty horse
He rolled me on the ground
And so I said "Well, that is that"
And I sold him by the pound

For Anatole

The Woman Who Was Jealous of God

And I loved her with my soul
And worshipped her with my body
She all night within my arms
With her back curved within my belly
And she slept with depth
As I stood guard upon ourselves
With silent and internal satisfaction
And then upon the morn at table
Hours and hours of talk
With tea and coffee and bread of life
Then "Marry me and take me hence"
And I hesitated instinctive with Pavlovian recoil
From a place within unconscious and unknown
That had total power within my structure.
Thus I saw myself with automatic retreat
And I was dismayed at the force that drove me,
That the motor of my life
Was not from me but history.
I retreated forlorn, unknown unto myself
And she felt it
Before the thickness of a snowflake had
　　　separated us

Now the iron curtain of the soul had come
        between us
I excused with triviality
That I had damaged love before and
        never again
That geography was more than love
That work for each was necessary
That bread of life was needed
For bread of soul
But worse that mountains needed conquest
And by me for me
But no both she and I knew the falseness of me
And so perhaps the truth:
I cannot give myself to thee
Because I search for him that must be God
And I knew that forever I had changed
        the whole
Then she rose and came across the table
And with her hand
Did smite me across the face with mighty force
(As the Dane smote
The sledded Polacks on the ice)
A just response
From the woman who
Was jealous of God

Two Women

I ONCE caused the death of a woman; without malice, with kindness, but I caused her death, under my hand. I was performing a lumbar puncture since I thought the young mother had meningitis. But she had a tumour of the lining of the brain, which could have been cured by surgery, but which now pressed her brain into her spine since I had lowered the pressure below. "Should I have begun?"

"Yes, you'd do the same again".

To take action to save and in doing so to kill is the cruellest destiny. And that was the death of a woman.

One night I was called from my bed, unshaven, hair uncombed, shoelaces untied, white coat over pyjamas, running to save a life. Oh what wonder of destiny that I am he, who runs out of the night carrying the chance of life, and that the life of a woman. All was dark save her bed in white light. She was young, pale with eyes in unblinking terror, vomiting blood into the steel bowl, dark blue blood on polished steel. Nurse gave me the Sengstaken tube of brown rubber with a balloon at the end that I must inflate in her stomach to press on the bleeding veins.

"When I feed this tube down your throat try to swallow." I put my fingers in her mouth and blood rushed over my hand.

"I can't swallow it."

"Yes you can, you have to."

I sat on the bed, she with her arms around my shoulders, me with one hand behind her head, my other at her mouth. "Swallow, swallow now, swallow, go on, now swallow, swallow."

And we lived our moment of intensity. In the area of a lamp-lit bed we were one, struggling together, her arms around me, her blood over me. And then it was done and all was safe. And she looked at me from tearful eyes. "Who are you?"

"I'm the houseman," I replied.

Apple

THE YOUNGEST woman in my life was my step-daughter Pomme. We sat beside each other during the first movement of a string quartet in a concert of Haydn. She sat with intense interest and concentration, a spellbound little girl, for the first time experiencing a live string quartet. I felt her intensity and joy, but sat beside her knowing that my contact with her was nought compared to the potential I had to give to her. A gift that I had never revealed to her. A universe of flowing contact giving her kindness and warmth and enthusing her with my love of life, all never given, all trapped within my restless soul. I shared her delight as she discovered that Haydn is a love of freedom, a tool we can use to liberate our spirit.

I remembered how at the age of six she was beside me listening to Mozart's *Requiem*. I saw her uncover a great mystery and extend herself into a new dimension when she realised that the photographs of the singers in the programme were photographs of the soloists she saw upon the stage. The glance went from one to the other several times. I felt her understanding and joy in a self-extension she did not yet herself understand. She then not only wanted to hear but to see. She stood upon her seat and at the end jumped up and down clapping her little hands. But I observed all this and did not hug her close to tell her that she was not alone in what she felt. That the feeling brought about by music and great choirs was the best elicited from the hearts of men. I the man did not hold the child in human unity.

And now several years of life later she sat beside me dissecting out the plaited coloured ribbons of the string quartet, leaning forward to gain a few more inches of closeness to the stage. The first movement drew to its close and I felt her rising understanding that a plaiting and unplaiting of the ribbons was about to end, but in her innocence not knowing that there was a second movement. And I knew her knowing so that when at the last note her spontaneous racing hands came together, mine was there first, restraining the unique sound that would alone have filled the vast and wooden space at Snape. My left hand held her right for a piece of time, less than the size of an atom. And then she knew at once the greater structure within which her plaited ribbons lay. And with the resentment of a child she, a woman, recoiled her hand from mine.

V

DEATH WILL COME

Death will Come

And death will come,
And I will go.
From now till then
The precious time will flow away
Without me knowing
From where it comes
Or where it goes
Or how I should behave.
But will I die?
And if I do
What will remain?
And why should I wish
The thing that's left
To think of me
If I am gone
And none of me remains?

Montreal
14th October 1994

Finding Intimacy at Dinner

In a restaurant in Chelsea
I ate alone
Then commotion in the corner
A man lay on the floor
In pinstripe suit
Rigid, then moving rhythmically.
From my table
I moved rapidly around diners
In pairs and fours
Then in one practised move
I went to my knees
And took his shoulders
And rolled him
So his face was to the floor
Then in that moment urine appeared
As his epileptic fit took hold
I held his head
And examined his mouth
Around his clenched teeth
My knees now wet
With his urine
Then I consoled his smitten girl

"Don't worry, this will pass"
And now in control I look around
And forty diners ate their dinners
Maintaining etiquette and laughter
They tight within themselves
As I worked within their midst
I unseen, my dinner cooling
She frightened, "He never told me"
"It might be the first time" sez I
Then he started to recover
And in his daze I hold his hand
And I help him to his seat
Yes this has happened before
The ambulance had been called
By panicked waiters
So I write a letter
On the back of a menu
"Dear Doctor, the patient has suffered
A tonic clonic grand mal convulsion"
To be delivered by hand
To my distant and unknown colleague
Then last consolation to the girl
And I returned through the tables
The way I had come
Again unseen and unknown
My ignored dinner now was cold

Being a victim of association
In payment of my bill
I gave no tip
But walked with sticky knees
Towards the door
Through the general denial of the world

ICELAND

From the skipper of a Grimsby trawler
In January Icelandic seas
I heard on the BBC
The relay of transmission
By short-wave wireless
"Gale-force 8, icing severe
For fifteen hours
We can't hold her any longer
We'll be going over soon
Operator say goodbye to our families
The crew send their love to their wives
It'll be soon,
We're going, we're going now
We're going over, we're going over"
And the understanding of destiny
Spread from the Icelandic storm
To me a youth on land

On recalling the BBC news heard in my youth
August 2003

The Death of the Priest

INTERACTION with leaders of other disciplines is invigorating. I had been sitting at a large table in a great white room with Georgian windows of massive yet delicate proportion, with men who were leaders in subjects different from my own, yet beautiful and deep, full of tradition and application and analysis of the human condition from diversely coloured angles. I was with the Professors of Law, War Studies, Spanish, Music, Physics, Education, and Pharmacology, each an engine of human discovery. We debated how we could measure the relative quality of research between the subjects. Oh what a wonderful analysis of what is important to understanding. Should we hire a satellite to photograph the missile sites in South Africa or should we buy a rare manuscript of Handel? Should we fund research in Sickle Cell disease or buy computers for linguistic analysis?

I left the committee room fulfilled, congratulating myself, smiling inwardly. At the end of the corridor a notice: "Catholic Mass, one o'clock". I looked at my watch, it was three minutes to one. I'd been caught. In academic complacency I'd been found, held by the lapels of my jacket and shaken. When challenged, accept. There is no other possibility. To retreat is not to understand that evolution requires a leap.

Instead of turning right down the great stairs, I turned left into the Chapel, the Anglican Chapel, the Chapel at the Centre of the foundation of King's as the Academic Church of England in London, at the centre of the College founded by the Anglican Church, over which Wellington had fought a duel when accused of consorting with Catholics. And there in the middle of the Chapel a Catholic altar. Its original placing must have been a great step in evolution. I knelt on the back row of concentric circles of benches and heard Mass. Fifty students wore jeans and t-shirts. I wore a tie. They all went to communion. I did not. They were relaxed and adjusted to the judgement of God. I was not. They could compromise. I could not. But perhaps I misjudged them, perhaps they were all in a state of grace, unlike me.

The priest went straight to the door of the chapel after Mass to greet his flock. As I stood in line for my handshake I knew he was interested in me; I, unique in the tie and blue suit carrying the briefcase stuffed with papers.

"Father Jennings."

"Professor Martin."

"Oh, I did not know we had a Professor who was a Catholic."

"A bad Catholic, Father, but not quite as bad as Graham Greene," I quoted.

He incised my history and character, learning quickly that I had studied mediaeval philosophy in Spain before medicine. "Good, I'm having trouble with applying the principle of double effect to death in modern medicine."

"I have no problem," sez I. "Have lunch with me and we'll discuss it."

He was conservative, empathetic, intelligent and active. He enjoyed his role. He stood high and straight in the Gothic chasuble at the top of the Anglican steps at King's. As Anglicanism had retreated into compromising self-doubt with social work replacing theology, this man had told me what he needed: an explanation from the philosophically trained Professor of Medicine of the principles of Aquinas applied to the genetically engineered foetus. "I'm the man," my arrogance declared, but within an instant I felt a jaggedness in my stomach as fear of dishonesty overwhelmed my knowledge that I was the man.

How could I, who could not receive communion because I was living in adultery, in a mess of marriage that was valid and invalid, annulled and unannullable, civil and canonical, transient and eternal, fertile and infertile, all consummated in the flesh and not in the mind; how could I bring philosophy and medicine together for this innocent priest? I writhed on those main stairs. I heard again the Monseigneur, Chairman of the Diocesan Tribunal asking me how much I had been committed to my marriage vows. I replying that I presumed that marital commitment had a Gaussian distribution throughout the world's population and that I lay within two standard deviations of the mean.

He was not amused, even confused. I asked to see my wife's statement, he said that was not allowed. I told him that offended natural justice, again he was confused but after a telephone call to Rome, he agreed. All this seen in my mind before I reached the foot of those tolerant Anglican stairs. Where did tolerance become mediocrity? When was application of principle too rigid? What was hypocrisy? What was I?

I turned and looked back up the stairs at Father Jennings, public schoolboy accent, Catholic Priest working uncompromisingly in Anglican headquarters. He knew who he was.

At the lunch I plunged straight into icy waters.

"Go to communion if you want to; I don't see the problem," was his simple and direct solution.

"But principle, and natural law and scandalising others," I replied.

"But the love of God," he finished the problem.

Who was more subtle, deep, him or me? Who really understood, him or me? Who was honest, him or me? Whose action was the right one, his or mine?

He had a simple straight solution, which he proclaimed, there in the Archduke Wine Bar, in Roman Collar drinking my Chablis, a contented and powerful integration of himself, the world and God. I, troubled, believing that there was about a sixty-five percent probability that the best hypothesis to explain the origin of the universe included a God with personality, and having to invoke Aristotle's definition of moral certainty to justify my attitude, and believing that action should be driven by reason. I left all this unsaid as I refilled his glass from a bottle marked "Premier Cru" which we both agreed had value.

Generously he gave me his past. He had read English Literature in Cambridge, then studied to be an Anglican priest at King's! He had left dissatisfied and became the tutor to the children of the Sultan of Sharjan in the Persian Gulf. He revelled in his role of teacher in the feudal system. He had then become a Catholic priest and later studied church history at Cambridge. He was a man of diversity like myself, yet his external diversity was supported by internal singularity. I was diverse inside and out. He was happy, I was not.

The bottle of Premier Cru lay inverted in the ice bucket. I perceived with unease a new facet to his personality. Was his manner now a little lighter than before? Did I sense that he might not have felt a need to love a woman? Did I, through some unrecognised antenna, perceive that we were different? Could this have a bearing on our mutually exclusive solutions to complexity versus simplicity, to unity and diversity? For less than a moment I allowed the beginning of the question of whether his solution to my problems might harbour the need for self-justification in a way that would never affect me. But I dismissed even the threshold of my judgement or misjudgement in honour of this man of God.

With professionalism we discussed the teaching of the ethics of death to medical students. I promised to arrange his inclusion in the course and we parted after a rare meeting. I wrote to the Dean explaining how appropriate was Father Jennings to be included with the long-haired general practitioner in the teaching of ethics. The Deanery responded as all Deans do in confusion: no reply. I neglected my undertaking and time passed.

Then in the College Newsletter I read his obituary. Derek Jennings was dead. My first thought came from fear: a man of my age was dead. But why? I read again, there was no mention of a justifying motor accident. And then a deformity in the flow of life, in the order and continuity of things. A hammer blow far away whose vibration hurts the skin.

The thought I had suppressed before returned. Had this man preached one thing and done another? Was his liberality generated by the necessity of self-justification? Was this man a hypocrite? Had he died of AIDS?

And for days I carried the problem unresolved, uncompleted, causing me confusion. I relied on my imperfect diagnostic skills without having read the autopsy report. Had he turned something beautiful and ancient into a contradiction? Had he betrayed me by his priestly virtue as I struggled before him mana-cled and chained by my failure to do what the church asked me to do? Was he a hypocrite? I had applied the imperfect possibility of my medical judgement to a single whole unique man who need not justify him-self to anyone save himself (and God if he so wished). Who was the hypocrite, Derek Jennings or John Martin?

The funeral had passed. It was attended by the Cardinal and Bishops both Catholic and Anglican, but not by me. I claimed diplomatic immunity: my patients needed me. Then the memorial service, which was to be held in the Chapel of King's, where I had first heard him say Mass. This was too much of a coincidence — the magic of a repetition, unexpected, unprepared yet calling, overcame my reticence born of prejudice, unintended yet inhibitory. I entered the Chapel for the Mass, embarrassed with myself I knelt beside the Professor of French, a fascinating man who combined an interest in translating French mediaeval love poetry with an expertise on the French Right between the wars.

I could not resist: "How did he die?" I whispered.

"Oh I'd have thought you would have known. It was leukaemia. And he refused all treatment so that he could accept destiny and fully experience his death. He died during the Gloria of a Mass celebrated by the Cardinal in his room."

Oh what nobility of spirit I had misjudged. I had not only lowered him in my mind, but worse, failed to see his light. I was the hypocrite. I had betrayed him, not him me. I became elated that justice had been done to Father Jennings. I was liberated from a poorer part of me.

The Anglican choir sang Mozart while communion was distributed. "If you are not a Catholic do not receive communion, but come to the altar for an affirmation." A line of academics in front of me approached the altar, each bowing for a blessing with the hand of the priest upon his head. When it came to me again the priest assuming I was a heretic automatically placed his hand upon my head.

"No Father, I'm a Catholic."

His hand took the bread from the golden bowl and put the body of Christ in my mouth.

I had learned from Father Jennings.

Death of Man

SOME weeks are flat, the only change being the progression of time. Others are like a boiling cauldron when change upon change occurs in the life of man, disproportionate to the effect of time. The evolution of mountains and animals from the beginning probably has not happened in a continuous line, but massive change has occurred in short steps of time producing a new glacier over a hundred years that will progress with infinite slowness for ten hundred thousand years, or a new blood cell in a year of change that lasts for half a million.

If we live on the products of what has gone before, we must mirror the system of evolution in some way, even within an individual's personal journey. Perhaps death is the ultimate jump in the equilibrium of evolution. But if a human being is more than biological evolution and has some free control over himself, then he must recognise the signs that the avalanche has begun. In an instant he must feel that the gathering wave is building energy for him so that he makes the choice to surf with sails goose-winged down the advancing face of water to be carried effortlessly for miles, instead of heading the prow directly into the breaking surf and with one massive effort overcoming the power of the wave, but staying exactly where he is.

On Monday morning before eight I took the underground to Baker Street to meet a psychologist to start discussions about the possibility of considering whether psychoanalysis was something that was enhancing or just a stupidity. I knew in my heart that there were layers of me within to be uncovered; that my personality although big and colourful was just a scraping from the surface of the bark of a tree that had roots intertwined with those of other trees in dank, damp earth deep below. And above green leaves in blue sky. And the whole tree was me.

But I denied it. There was no scientific experiment to test the value of psychoanalysis. She did not parry my aggressive thrust, but acquiesced, "Of course," with a smile. Was not modern psychoanalysis derived from the commercial organisation set up by Freud?

"That is a criticism," she agreed, but she was from the Jungian School.

"Tell me about that."

Jung said that dreams were a window into the sub-conscious man, they were a language that had to be learned if you were to read the hidden causes within.

"But surely this could be simply nocturnal electrical storms within the brain, having no meaning."

"Perhaps," she smiled.

"I had a very strange dream last night." I found myself revealing my first nakedness to her (or perhaps to me). "I was in a shallow valley and my wife was walking away from me along the ridge that made the side of the valley. I called to her repeatedly, 'Patricia', but that was not her name. When I woke I could not understand why I should call my wife by a name that wasn't hers."

"It must mean something."

"No."

"Jung would say it must have meaning for you."

"But I don't know a Patricia and it has no meaning, perhaps it just means I don't communicate with her."

Then it struck. A new and total understanding coming from some unknown place. Obviousness, vision and relief occurred together in an instant. Patricia was a feminine from *Pater*, the Latin for Father. My father had just died. I was calling him to stay. But why to my wife?

Then the second realisation came. She was like my father. Her quiet introverted weaknesses were the same as my father's. I had the same feeling of protection to that part of both of them. Was this in part why I loved her, why I felt I could not let go? Would losing my wife be like losing my father? Patricia, father and wife in Latin. It rang true, but where within me was this made? I might have lived all my life without knowing this obvious thing.

Walking back to Baker Street station I felt enhanced, liberated, wiser, relieved. But this was one word understood. Were there a thousand? Was there an ancient internal world that influenced me without my knowing? Or was I simply a very well organised neural network with such excess capacity that "Patricia" was simply a meaningless short circuit?

My father had died the week before. I was sitting at my desk dealing with an unremembered, unnecessary triviality. The phone rang. My brother said, "Dad's collapsed — it sounds serious."

"Pulmonary embolus?" questioned I.

"Could be," said he with guilt at inappropriate professionalism. We two, trying not to be like doctors but like sons, rushing across England to be with him before the end.

I walked into the ward where I had once worked, in the hospital where I had seen dozens of deaths. I saw through a window the hospital in which my father had been born, in which I had been born and in which I had delivered babies, this was a place of happening. "I am his son," I told the nurses, omitting titles that were trivial at this time. Every muscle and tendon was taught and prepared for the awful truth that he was already gone.

"Your brother is already here."

"That means he must still be alive," I convinced myself, not wanting to know yet if it were not true.

The nurse led me to my father. There he was, breathing as though fighting, his eyes staring or unseeing, none could say except he who could not say. My brother spoke to me as doctor to doctor about pyrexia and cyanosis and jugular venous pressure. I thought, "Don't, it's our Father," but I took part in the evasion of our true feelings and replied in words of blood oxygen and cerebral perfusion.

Then we saw the doctor of the father of the doctors and we three played the game of professionalism with smiles and thanks. We made a covenant that Dad should be allowed to die without machines and devices and electronics to hinder his path. And we behaved and danced around each other. Then to my father's side.

My uncle arrived. He the priest. Tu es sacerdos in aeternum, and you function ex opere operator. He too assumed his profession with the prayers for the dying. But this profession was different. It took no pay, it was not measurable by science, but came from a deep and distant part with a power that was undiminished when science was finished and medicine exhausted.

Then the litany of the saints: "All ye holy saints and angels", "pray for him," the sons replied, "St Augustine" "pray for him", "Saints Cosmos and Damian" "pray for him", "Saints Peter and Paul" "pray for him", "St Cuthbert" "pray for him", "St Anastasia" "pray for him", "St Francis" "pray for him". And we four became joined by a covenant that was between us. A reality between father and sons, brother and brother, sons and father. And the thought of the blood gas concentration became trivial. We were joined and that thing between us lived. "All ye holy patriarchs and prophets" "pray for him", "St Gregory" "pray for him".

I held my Father's right shoulder and my brother his left hand. "St Cecilia" "pray for him" and we asked a Roman virgin, player of the harp to greet our father, "St Martin" "pray for him". And a Roman soldier of great charity was called upon. "St Thomas More" "pray for him". And with us was the greatest Englishman.

"Don't be afraid, we are here with you," my brother spoke into my father's ear. I, given courage comforted, "Do not worry about the children, we will look after them."

"There is nothing to be frightened of, we're all here." "St Luke" "pray for him", "St Mark" "pray for him".

"He's in ventricular fibrillation." My brother retreated for a moment back into the shell of medicine, but in the next breath was again the greater reality. "Kyrie Eleison, Christe Eleison."

An enormous gasp and I held his shoulder tighter: "There is nothing to fear, Dad." "He's dying, Uncle," from my brother. "Receive his soul all ye angels of heaven." And the tears ran down the face of my brother; my strong and reserved brother was crying. And my father did not breathe but his hand was warm. "Goodbye," my brother said. "In Paradisum perducant te Angeli." And the priest's faith was a massive rock.[12] My brother gave me his handkerchief that was wet with his tears.

And the cement was now between the three of us alone. I could not feel my father as one of us, but his shoulder was still warm. And I stood and stood and could not leave. "Say goodbye," my brother told me.

"I can't," said I.

"Come on," he pulled my arm.

And away we walked. There had been four of us, and now there were three and I did not understand where my father was.

As I walked down the corridor I again looked over

to the hospital in which he was born, and I remembered the complementary lack of understanding twenty years before, in the hospital I could now see from my father's deathbed, when I had delivered a baby for the first time. Then I had not understood from where the child had come that slipped into my hands. There had been the mother, the midwife and me. Then in a moment there had been four of us. In amazement I held the child not understanding. Now I did not understand where my father had gone.

The Death of the Black Rider

MY FATHER had died the week before. I arose full of heavy introversion. I was next in line. Even the morning shower was dull. I was using up that time that I now realised was my only currency.

I changed lanes sadly, without my usual competition for the best position at the traffic lights. Turning into a wide boulevard I perceived an irregularity of structure somewhere ahead to the right. Things were not usual. However, I changed lanes and moved to my left turn. Then for a moment, a smudge the size of a micron, on the retina of my eye, something black and long perceived upon the outside of my vision where the eyeball is close to my nose.

As I turned the car left I threw my head right and for a moment saw the black rider. Lying long, extended low on the ground, languid, pre-Raphaelite, all black, alone, isolated, utterly original, different from all else. I perceived a halo of standing men radiating from him, curving at the edges, as they bowed left and right towards him. I'd completed my turn. The arguments of my self-pity arose: I was late for the meeting, I'd had enough tragedy this week, it was a no-parking area. Oh how can man be seduced by such triviality? Stop! I was a special man, I could change things, I was a leader, I was a doctor.

I left the car open and ran back into the boulevard. I now had become professional: don't run too fast otherwise your performance will be impaired on arrival for those important seconds of judgement that will determine the next minutes of action. Traffic gave way to me as I moved forward towards him lying long and black in the gutter. Extended, elegant, soft black leather on thin languid arms by his side, his head in black helmet with black visor. An unknown man was within. Three men stood above him, but at a distance. Each with a mobile telephone held to his head, each bending slightly to look at him, but from a distance as though forbidden to approach a sacred sacrifice, consoling themselves that they were doing something by manipulating the electronics of their trivial world while he died before them. Then I was with him. Oh what a tragic man. Encased in one sheet of black leather and helmet and black visor with blood running onto the road from between the black helmet and black jacket. Black and red like an anarchist flag.

I put my fingers into the tiny space between helmet and jacket. He was warm. There was the sternomastoid, but there was no carotid pulse. Oh my God! His heart has stopped and I am all alone, with the gravel of the road hurting my knees through my blue suit trousers. My other hand went between his black glove and sleeve. His wrist was warm as though he had risen from bed, but there was no pulse.

"Don't touch him" — I heard a scream from the crowd. A woman consoling herself by doing something she had heard might help, justifying her hysterical and ignorant inactivity.

"I'm a doctor." I was in command of life and death. Start his heart. I thumped my fist upon his chest.

"Oh no, oh no!" I heard a man shout, as he who was involved realised with gripping awfulness that the rider was going to die. Still no pulse and I had been there for perhaps eight seconds. Check the time: nine twenty-one. The helmet must come off: the site of haemorrhage, airway access and the state of his pupils. Under an unseen chin I found a complicated opening device that I could not open. I was still alone. I turned to a man with a mobile telephone: "Stop a rider with a helmet and bring him here." In a second moment a face with a big moustache said, "Press and turn like this," showing me his own helmet. He was a good man, I had seen his face only for a flash, but I knew him, he was part of our team and we had not yet seen the man.

The lock opened, I eased the bleeding helmet and the black clad mystery was gone and a human being revealed. But his face was dead. His pupils were still small, he had living brain, but the look upon his face was death. Quick, quick, the heart.

I ripped the jacket open, then the shirt, buttons flying. I smelt the soap he had used an hour before. Punch, punch, punch, my hand squeezing his heart to pump. Quick the time: nine twenty-two. Oh help me God, I have nothing, no equipment. I cannot stop, Where is the source of haemorrhage? How am I to ventilate his lungs? And then the team grew. "I've got an airway, I'm a first-aider." Oh what beauty and simplicity. He knelt beside me, placing one plastic end behind the rider's tongue and the other into his own mouth, blowing rhythmically. Unknown men united in such intimacy that only God is closer. "Well done," he shared his breath with the rider.

The pupils were still small, his brain living in its depths, but again I saw there was no life in this face. Oh help me, I need equipment. We were isolated, alone, a band of men fighting for a man because he was a man, holding him with us by the thinnest margin. Then the strength of our society grew. A green motorbike was stopping with green leathers and then without a word in one soft gentle movement of lighted steel and plastic tube the green rider had intubated the man and fresh air was flowing into his lungs. At last a colleague, a comrade.

"Well done," I greet him and we grinned at each other in relaxed professionalism.

"I'm a Professor of Medicine from King's, do you have an ECG on your bike?"

"Yes, I'll get it." Time: nine twenty-three-and-a-half. I turn my head and the first eyes I meet I say, "Come here and squeeze this bag like this."

"OK but I was driving the red van."

"It doesn't matter, squeeze the bag." I'm still pumping. In my right field of vision black motorcycle boots and black trousers — a policeman.

"Can you do this?"

"I'll try."

He takes my place and after three seconds of tuition, my hands on his, he is an expert. I feel the femoral pulses and, yes, we have blood circulating. I sit on my haunches to re-assess. Air — OK, heart — OK, bleeding from the nose and mouth — nothing to be done. The quiet green clad man is setting up the ECG.

"All stop," say I and on the screen a flat line of death. "Start again."

Oh God help us, I the one who does not believe in prayer was praying. And the prayer was answered. "The helicopter's coming from 'The London'," I was told by an unknown policeman in my ear, and almost immediately I heard the clipped clatter of distant helicopter blades banging on the air. Somewhere above an angel flew, bringing us all we desired. Oh what wonderful relief, we were not alone, our team extended into the sky. I looked and there it was, still high, turning slowly, but with us.

I, back to examining my patient, found the pupils were now bigger. The last of the brain was dying. How long? — time nine twenty-five. And then the beauty of order arrived; two helicopter surgeons in orange suits, striding through the crowd, equipment bags on shoulders, confident, powerful, with focused movement. "This is a Professor of Medicine from King's," the green rider told them.

"There is no need to say that," I said.

"It's important we know who we are," he replied.

Effortlessly the structure of our job, and rank and training descended on us and my loneliness was gone. Knives cut veins, warm plasma was pumped, electricity applied, "Do you have adrenaline?"

"We still have good output."

"What sort of career structure do you have?"

"We are surgical registrars awaiting senior posts."

With ease, lubricated by years of training, we combined humour with discussion about precision operations. "Examine his skull" and my fingers felt the broken eggshell of his head. "It's fragmented on the right." And within a moment all had changed and the direction of the world was different. His pupils were large and fixed, and blood came uncontrollably from his mouth and nose.

"That's enough," I said, "let's pack it in," using the slang of my junior doctor days. And we all stood around the unknown man who was dead, a great team who had given time and place and power because he was a man. (When I told the story to a Spanish doctor, that they would even send a helicopter to a rider lying in the gutter he said, "This is a sign of a noble society.")

Time nine thirty-five, we were comrades who had worked together. "I'll cover him with a blanket from the ambulance." There were fifteen or twenty fighters for his life. We chatted with warm friendship, washed our hands of his blood in helicopter alcohol.

"What time did he die, doctor? The Coroner will want to know," said the policeman with the "book".

"Nine twenty-nine." The decision was made.

I sat in my car, my hands sticky on the wheel with the last of his blood and I cried for him. There in my car I said goodbye to my father knowing his death had been right and free. The rider had been lost before he could know himself. And still as I drive down that boulevard there are each day fresh flowers upon the tree beside where he died. A sign of love unfulfilled.

Later I received this letter:

Dear Professor Martin

With regard to the accident you witnessed your statement was accepted and read at the Coroner's Court. Your help in this unfortunate matter is much appreciated by both the family who have had to accept there was no one else at fault and myself. Thank you. A verdict of Accidental Death was recorded by the Coroner.

Yours sincerely

John Slater
Police Sergeant

Death in Kerry

H E WAS in the big bar when I went to drink my
first pint of Guinness. I do not know that I
saw him, but I might have. I was never to know him,
but his death was to touch me gently at the edges of
my life while I was in Kerry. The bar was packed with
tourists and Kerrymen, with precise gentle Dutchmen,
brown legs in shorts, and with ancient farmers in
tweed jackets and a rim of white skin at the top of the
forehead where their habitual outdoor caps protected
them from the weather.

I had returned to Ireland for the first time in years
to rediscover the human and physical beauty that I
had forgotten. Kerry amazed me. Strangers greeted
me for no other reason than human warmth. I saw
vistas that were alchemies of mountain, sea and sand.
I was the only one gazing upon them. Thick slices of
natural things accompanied by black beer, whisky,
coffee and cream were fed me.

On Sunday in Dingle, the previous Irish Prime
Minister could be distinguished as the one with

creases in his trousers. He climbed onto the lorry and spoke charming words about fishing and the West to the hundred of us standing on the new harbour to watch the annual races of the small black skin-covered boats in which Irishmen have ridden the waves for the last 2000 years. I watched very young men with innocent faces pound the sea with round poles. Then to Sleah Head. I left the car and walked the mile over the last rump of Ireland. Over grass fine as a lawn till I was the last person in the West in Europe. Sea crashed left, right and in front of me. I noticed there was still one rabbit further west than me. Then along came two Italian students I had given a lift to earlier. "What do you study?" I asked one.

"Theology," was the answer from the hippy-bearded, ear-ringed student.

"Do you believe in God?"

"No," came the answer from the Theologian.

"Then who caused the Big Bang?" asked I.

"You should know, you're the scientist."

"Then perhaps God is hydrogen," said I. I moved a few paces east and the atheist became the most westerly man in Europe.

The back of the hotel in Glenbeigh looked onto the front door of the church. I realised that I could sit in bed sipping tea and if I squinted, I could see the high altar and so be "morally present" at Mass. I went down to breakfast, ordered the whole feast, then walked to Lyon's shop to buy the Irish Times. Then, with my mouth full of bacon, egg and soda bread, I read that he had died on Saturday night. Drowned on the beach below the hotel in the night after we had drunk together in the bar. He was twenty-three. Drowned on the beach where I had swum. Drowned on the beach of amazing beauty, infinitely long and wide, where great plates of thin, clear water rushed across the lateral sand.

That evening as I returned from fishing the best salmon pool on the lower Caragh River, I could not find a place to park the car. I perceived men with ties and white shirts and women with dresses moving to a compass point. I looked in the church and saw a hundred kneeling and praying. I asked in the hotel what was happening. It was the wake. At dinner I knew his body lay forty yards away.

I slept late. My right arm and back stiff from casting over an infertile pool. I squinted out of my window. The front wall of the church was lined with men, wishing to take part but not daring to go in, probably all in mortal sin like myself. I knew it must be the requiem mass. As I shaved I remembered the beauty of "Dies irae, dies illa, solvet saeclum in favilla, Teste David cum Sybilla", then to my breakfast feast.

The second day on the lower Caragh I walked the

bank. This was prize enough. To have cast my spinner a dozen times beside the very rock where Patsy O'Grady told me the biggest of the salmon rested was total fulfilment. To have not caught a salmon was ecstasy. The fish of Kings should remain a mystery, uncaught. That night in the dining room, all was human friendship as usual. I was told I might have to wait longer for my dinner (what did I care?) as there were so many people to be served in the public bar after the requiem mass. I was content sipping my Guinness and waiting to be called. I was taking part in the right rhythm of things. A rhythm I had lost.

On the last day, after I had ridden an Irish horse across the sands, I returned sweating and aching to my centre of gravity, that fifty yards between the hotel and the church. Three hundred people stood facing towards its open door. Some men in tight tweed jackets, ties and caps, younger men in jeans and pullovers. And in their midst, two embarrassed Germans in plastic shorts and t-shirts sitting outside the pub drinking Guinness and reading their maps unsure where to look or how to behave in the action of deep reality. The door of the main bar was closed for the first time since I was there. The barman stood his guard of respect outside it. The bell of the church rang and all the hundreds as one made the sign of the cross. I too could not resist the ancient call. The coffin emerged carried by the dead man's brothers down the small hill past us all. The policeman stopping all traffic saluted without embarrassment. As the coffin passed me towards its grave in the alchemy of beauty, I again crossed myself. A deep longing within showed me what I had given up for my life in London.

Kerry, 1992

THE DEATH OF THE WOMAN

M Y FATHER had died as a victim of the world, innocent and vulnerable, hit by a motorcar while taking to the bank the cheque I had sent him. On the other hand, even at her death my mother had been in control. She had lain in a hospital bed tended by her beloved nuns for several weeks, glorying in the incapacity that centred her in a world from which she had always reaped gratification. And in doing this she showed courage. (For what is courage but action to achieve that, which is not normally possible, but is desired?)

My uncle, the priest, told me he would say Mass in my mother's room and asked if I would choose and read the epistle. That was easy. I chose the same as I had chosen for my wedding Mass: the Roman centurion confronting Christ as he might have confronted his general if he thought the strategy were wrong. He was asking for the healing of his daughter, which Christ at first refused. But in granting her life Christ was saying to the soldier that there are more important things than the death of a child, such as those things that bind us together in life, like faith, (and faith I knew had use and meaning even in my world of molecular dissection of the cell). And my mother had faith, which produced a power that she now exercised in her semi-coma.

The Mass began, my uncle bringing the powers of Latin ages to the bed, Ex opere operator, power undiminished by his frailty. As I read the words of Christ spoken to the Roman soldier, spoken now to my dying mother, her breathing grew faster. I, the doctor, did not intervene. I finished my reading and my uncle took the place of Christ as I took my mother in my arms and stroked her hair, knowing she was about to die. And at the moment of consecration, when my uncle made the bread of God within his hands, one last breath happened, and I knew there would be no more, not from the evidence that they had not occurred, but from knowing this was the end.

I laid her back upon the pillow as my uncle continued his act of infinite value, which did not stutter for a moment at the death of my mother, and nuns appeared, eight or ten entering the room, knowing with a nunly sense. Mass finished with one less of us than when I had read the epistle. And the nuns as naturally as a football crowd, sang their own anthem. There, my mother had done it. She had achieved what she desired.

DEATH OF A PATIENT

ASSISTING at my first surgical operation, I was introduced to a world of magic, of an intensity of green under strong light, of silver metal against pink bowel. A world where I was stripped of all previous human experience, like an Arctic explorer viewing the all-enveloping ice and snow, where nothing from his past could be perceived, no house, no land, no person.

So the operating theatre was terra incognita. Men had eyes, and wore green gowns and masks. We stood elevated on pedestals as though at a fire step in a war or before an altar. On my fingers was a fine and gorgeous instrument that clicked deliciously as I clipped it round a tiny spot of spouting blood, intensely red in the focused light. This was not just the work of some elite regiment or arcane priesthood, it was a noble but secret pursuit of man; exclusive, important beyond understanding. It gave me a purpose undreamt of.

I stood in the line of men scrubbing hands and arms, using brown liquid iodine, silent with only eyes above masks to communicate that we were leaving

normal life. I loved this radical and beautiful experience, this liberating world where one could start again,
using a flowing natural vigour that normal life kept
trapped under pressure deep within. As a houseman I
had been fulfilled as never before, driving my destiny,
but running with others, using every part of my being,
working day and night and day, using hand and eyes
and mind, and with joy.

Oh what fulfilment! To receive the call at ten
o'clock at night from a lonely doctor fifty miles away
who feared the approaching night. Where patient lay
in the darkened ward with blood pressure dropping
and the pulses in his legs decreasing. He had put off
the dreadful possibility since afternoon. Perhaps it
was intestine that was twisted that would right itself,
perhaps infection with the fever yet to appear. In early
evening he had seen the blood pressure start to drop
as the abdominal pain increased. Perhaps this was a
punctured bowel that he himself should operate on in
his small fishing town. But all was not clear within his
dedicated yet troubled mind. He did again what he
was trained to do. Kneeling by the bed in the darkened ward he had placed his right hand upon the man
and felt the line of pain deep within. And the thought
came.

He saw in his mind blood leaking from the great
vessel and tracking within the structure of its wall.

In an automatic instant he felt the pulses of the arteries of the legs. And he knew it now with certainty. He saw the whole picture in his mind, the hundred confusing possibilities gave way to one: a bleeding aortic aneurysm. But instead of fulfilment, his searching confusion gave way to great loneliness. This man before him had given him all his trust, all his belief, and his life was flowing away with his unseen blood within. He did not have the skill or the equipment, or the team, or the theatre, or the pints of blood or the support. He stood in a quiet and lonely fear. A fear he had to face alone. His chief was now ten miles away snoozing after an over-large whisky. He feared his chief. He feared the decision. Was this the end of life? Was the good decision for this man and for the darker world outside to let him die? He feared the conversation with the patient's wife: "If we had been elsewhere, perhaps." And all this in the moment of the rising from his kneeling examination.

The only solution he knew for fear was truth. "If you stay with me then you will die." But said over five minutes with sensitive probing for response and understanding of confusion and taking responsibility to mould the decision in the direction that was right. Yes, taking responsibility to know what the other should know. And this was not manipulation or irresponsible use of power, but generosity in giving in minutes what he had received in years.

"I'll phone my colleagues." And he was not alone, and fear was unperceived. Out of his darkness he was united with all those pools of light in the growing night where his friends signalled to each other with eyes, that things were going well, or that more blood was needed.

Two minutes later he spoke to me, I sitting on my bed in my attic room above the ward. The hospital telephonist, desiring to be involved, introduced: "It's Grimsby General, Doctor." Excitement tensed muscles as I knew that something difficult and great was to come into my hands. I had no fear. I knew that whatever message came through fifty miles of darkness I was the man that would say "yes", I would lead my world to fulfilment in doing what we do.

"I've spoken to Doncaster and they can't do it."

"Send him straight away."

"Thank you, I'll order the ambulance and send his wife with him; I'll ask the police for an escort."

"What's his blood group?"

"O positive."

"Good." And I took responsibility for the unseen man, for the tiredness of my colleagues in the morning, for the thirty pints of O positive blood even now reserved with his name on them, for the distant hope of his wife gripping his white hand as they crossed the flat and darkened Yorkshire plain, for the young policeman on his motorbike in the rain flying ahead to stop the traffic at the next junction, wet whistle in wet mouth, below wet face, splashed by the racing ambulance as it passed the red traffic light, all held safe by the policeman's flashing blue. And then flying forward again passing the ambulance to hold safe the next obstruction. He and I, unknown to each other, linked by the nobility of our calling: to serve an unseen man because he was a man.

"It's less than fifty-fifty," I tell his wife, "but I promise you he will have everything that can be given." After five hours of operating my senior registrar is struggling. I see the sweat around his eyes that meet mine for a part of a moment to signal distress. We had not spoken for half-an-hour. I automatically responding deep in the abdomen to his needs. And now this man has fear. "I can't do it, the stitches won't hold." He will not again signal with his eyes. "Let's try again, change places." And again he struggles within the man he has not met, because of my word to my dark and distant colleague by telephone. I transferred the fear of one to the fear of the other.

An hour later, "I still can't do it, I'll have to take the aortic clamp off." And again those eyes to mine.

"I can't see what else you can do. We have used twenty-eight pints of blood and we have none in reserve." This was my help to him. This was my small help with his responsibility.

The man was living, with blood pumping from his heart. "Blood pressure stable", from the anaesthetist removed from our decisions, speaking from some distant engine-room. And my senior registrar opened the aortic clamp. And it was right. It was the most right and the most dreadful thing. The blood that we had given the man filled the space between the senior registrar and me. "Blood pressure gone," we heard upon the telegraph. And the man died.

I went straight to his wife. "We did everything we could": simple, trite, oft repeated, but good and right. She consoled by my strength and honesty, I taking my strength from her, because she was his wife.

Then the best of all. I sat in the changing room with my senior registrar, just before the break of a wet and gloomy dawn, smoking a cigarette. Still in green, in old armchairs, beaten and worn by such use, our feet on the arms of each other's chair. Our white Wellington boots covered in the blood of that man and a dozen others whose blood was mixed with his, discarded on the floor. Tired and fulfilled we smoked our cigarettes.

CONTRADICTION IN DEATH

I KNOW with certainty of only one saint in my extended family. My wife's grandfather is surely in heaven if it exists, if it does not, he lives as an inspiration to me in a way that my grandfathers have not had the chance to be. He is in my martyrology. If you have the choice between being generous and not generous, be generous.

He was a soldier in the French army in the First World War. His regiment was in the trenches. A platoon had been ordered on a very dangerous mission. One of the platoon started to weep, saying to his comrades that he would certainly be killed. He pleaded that he was a poor man with five children. Who would provide for them when he was gone? My wife's grandfather, who was not ordered to go, volunteered to take the man's place, saying that he had one child (my mother-in-law) and that he was a rich man. He left with the platoon and was killed that night. The other man is now surely dead and his grandchildren living in a prosperous France. My grandfather-in-law would also be dead, as are my own grandfathers who fought in France. What matters is the generosity of that man. It is a contradiction to greed and mediocrity as great as that of the Cistercian monastery at Cluny, a novel by Saint-Exupéry or Saint-Saën's Third Symphony. We all have nobility within. Recognising nobility in others helps us recognise our own.

VI

THE ORIGIN OF LONELINESS

The Origin of Loneliness

And I thought Patagonia would be my friend
But no, it did not know me.
On the map there is nothing,
From the air a massive sameness
The land of loneliness
And I would know it
And it me
But No
On the road stood two eagles on the body
     of a hare
And around them a halo
Of other birds as beautiful as the dawn
And Patagonia was rich
And I was alone

El Calafate
11th April 2002

Loneliness

THE ETYMOLOGY of every word carries with it the history of the people speaking the language over tens of thousands of years. *Loneliness* is first found written in Hamlet (Etymology of the English Language, 1879, Rev W W Skeat, Oxford University Press), from *lone* first written in Henry IV, which is a short form of *alone*. (Another example of loss of the initial *a* is *mend*.) *Alone*: quiet by one's self. Middle English *al one* (*all one* in Modern English). *One* in Middle English was pronounced "own" to rhyme with "bone", this pronunciation is preserved in *loneliness*. c.f. Dutch *all-een*, German *all-ein* and late Old Icelandic *all-einna*.

Therefore loneliness carries with it the echo of wholeness, all one. And preserves, unknown to the speaker, a pronunciation of eight hundred years ago.

NOTES

1 (title page illustration) The church of St Mary, Market Square, Cracow, Poland. Pen and Ink. January 2002.

2 (p 28) First published in "The idea is more important than the experiment", The Lancet, 2000, volume 356, pp 934-937.

3 (p 34) "Chocolate" is derived from the Nalwatl "xocoatle", literally, bitter water. c.f. Joan Corominas *Breve diccio-nario etimológico de la lengua castellana*, Editorial Gredos 1973, Madrid. It is not connected with "xacáutl", cacao. c.f. *Chambers Dictionary of Etymology*, Chambers 1988, Edinburgh.

4 (p 57) During military exercises in the cold war NATO officers did not identify themselves over the radio by their personal names. This was to avoid Warsaw Pact forces, who listened to our transmissions, building up a picture of how individual officers moved within our land forces. Code names were therefore given to functions within a unit. A commanding officer was "Sunray". As a medical officer, my name was "Starlight".

5 (p 59) The parapet is the top of the trench facing the enemy over which a soldier has to leap when beginning

the attack. The fire step is the raised board on which the soldier stood to shoot over the parapet and from which he began his ascension over the parapet. Nothing in the breach: my grandfather told me that sometimes before an attack on the enemy trenches they were ordered to have no rounds in the rifle's breach that they could instantly fire, without spending time to action the bolt of the rifle: "nothing in the breach". They would have only the bayonet to fight with and therefore be encouraged to get to the enemy as quickly as possible using it as their only weapon. My family has served as soldiers in the East Yorkshire Regiment (or previously the XV Regiment of Foot), father and son, from the eighteenth to the twentieth centuries. I met an old man who had been a lieutenant in the 1st Battalion in 1917. He told me about the character of the soldiers in the East Yorks. They waited at dawn to go over the top to charge across three hundred yards of machine gun fire. He was proud that when he blew his whistle to go he need not look along the trench as he knew that every man would go.

6 (p 93) See p 102.

7 (p 94) While examining London University finals in Medicine a fellow examiner asked me (to enliven the repetitive tedium) if I had a solution to the problem of Zeno of Elea: when an arrow is shot to the target you can divide the time from any point in its flight in half and predict how much time it will take to reach the middle of its remaining flight from that point. This can be done infinitely so that the arrow will never reach the target.

But clearly the arrow does reach the target. The solution had to lie in an examination of the nature of the flight of the arrow (by "nature" Aristotle and Aquinas meant "that which makes it what it is"). Therefore, I suggested that the nature of the flight of the arrow contained indivisibility (Kant, Hume and Hegel also made comments on Zeno).

8 (p 100) John Duns Scotus was a medieval Scots philosopher who taught in Cambridge. If Duns had heard Haydn, he would have asked if the relationship between two notes had an existence independent of the notes themselves. He would have argued that it did since there was "something" (ie a difference) between the two notes as played and that was a different "thing" from any other relationship between any other two notes. These events on the edge of existence he called modalities.

9 (p 102) Francis Fukuyama's scholarly work, *The End of History and the Last Man* supposes that the purpose of man is organisational and economic. He asks whether we have achieved the Last Man, i.e. the final development (liberal democracy) beyond which there will be no further progress.

My view is that the state of organisational man is important but not the first question. Is not the nature of the state simply the substrate for man the individual and internal to use to achieve the fulfilment of the potential of his spirit? This can be done to a greater or lesser extent in any organisation system. However, some like the democratic socialist state, powered by liberal economics, make the job easier. Such organisational systems are therefore to be preferred, independently of any concept of justice. Man's potential is first achieved by the self-relationship, secondly by relationships with others. If this is accepted then the Last Man is within at the time of death. Fukuyama suggests that the progress of natural science is forming the Last Man. I suggest it is the availability of philosophy, art, music, and literature to all men that will help each approach the Last Man. And liberal democracy and natural science may be tools to achieve this end.

10 (p 116) *Come May You Sweet*, the title of a Danish folk song.

11 (p 134) *Usted* is the third person singular in formal address in Spanish. Literally a contraction of His Excellency. In Castillian, the third person is used in the formal respectful address. This has been lost in English. The French *vous* is less formal, being a second person address, even though it is plural. (In some Latin American countries, the third person is always used, even if the address is familiar.)

12 (p 167) I more and more understand the need for man to have a mystical structure to his life, for which biology and physics are simply a substrate.

Typeset in Adobe Garamond and Monotype Perpetua
Printed on Mohawk Superfine White Eggshell